CROSSING OVER AND BACK

A Grim Reaper Comedy Adventure

Riya Aarini

Crossing Over and Back: A Grim Reaper Comedy Adventure

ISBN: 978-1-956496-51-2 (eBook)

ISBN: 978-1-956496-52-9 (paperback)

www.riyapresents.com

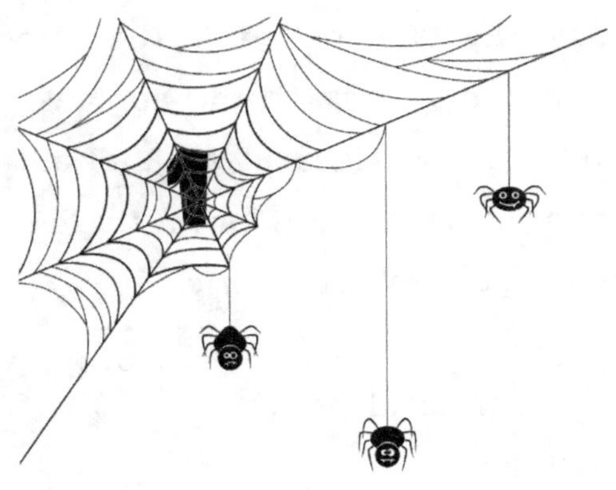

Another day, another slay.

After dropping off one more soul to the other side, I clicked my heel bones together and took a deep breath, centering myself and savoring the delicious moment. Then I paddled my boat back to the opposite shore, ready to pick up the next client on my continually replenishing list.

Carrying my shoulder bones back, I rubbed my fingerbones on my tattered black cloak and blew on them. A smile escaped my jawbone. I ought to win an Employee of the Year award for doing my job impeccably. As the only grim reaper on staff, I make a profound difference in the infinite afterlife of souls. Without me, how would they get the euphoric taste of eternity?

Just as I stepped off the boat with my skull high, my phone chirped.

“Hmm.” I wasn’t expecting anyone. Plus, the text message ringtone was different. It wasn’t the applause ringtone I’d set for Death’s text messages. I was, after all, a stellar employee deserving of recognition for my tireless work, day in, day out, for the past seven centuries.

Who could this be?

I plucked my phone from my cloak pocket.

It was Moe, the spirit guide.

Moe: Listen, Reaper, you need to return this soul to the world ASAP.

What?

I’d delivered my last client less than five minutes ago. Something had to be amiss. In my seven-hundred-years, I’d never misdelivered a soul. I had an exceptional track record, flawlessly bringing souls to the edge of the next world without a hitch. Precision was my game. I was a superstar transitioning the living to the eternal realm of the dead.

But now the spirit guide was asking me to return a soul? Bah.

I searched my phone for my list of clients, which Death had sent as a text attachment. Upon opening it, I checked it once, then twice. I let my skull fall back and let out a huge sigh. My last client was on the list, with his full name, date of death, and pickup location spelled out as clear as day.

Grumbling, I paddled my boat back to the banks of eternity.

As I approached, Moe stood on the fringes of the next world, arms hooked around the twig-like arm of the soul I'd just dropped off. The soul looked a little lost, almost angry.

"Hey, Moe. What's the deal?" I asked as soon as I was within hearing distance.

"Reaper, it's not his time. He needs to go back." Moe's voice sounded low and gruff. His frizzy, dirty gray beard laying against his mid-chest flapped as he spoke breathily through his thin lips.

It wasn't a voice I'd say no to. He was a spirit guide who worked closely with the Cosmic Light, ranking slightly higher than my boss, Death. In terms of hierarchy, the Cosmic Light took the C-Suite spot. He was the head honcho to whom Death, Life, and all other senior management reported.

"You sure?" I asked, despite not wanting to question my higher-up.

"No doubt about it." Moe pushed the soul back onto my boat. "Take him back."

"Okay." I didn't argue, but helped the soul get his bearings as he stumbled onto my boat, teetering on the still, deep river. Maybe it was just a minor administrative mix-up. No biggie. I'd return the soul to his earthly abode and be on my merry way.

As I paddled, the soul pressed his lips into a tight grimace. He sat slumped at the other end of my boat. With a heavy sigh, he began expressing his disappointment about being sent back.

"You know, Reaper, being on the other side was out of this world," he said, his once-gloomy expression starting to lighten.

"Well, that's because it literally is out of this world."

"No, you don't understand. The moment I stepped into eternity, I basked in unconditional love and an overwhelming joy I'd never felt on Earth." He spread his arms wide as he spoke, as if he were embracing the totality of the afterlife. His eyes gleamed.

"That's what they all say." Throughout my career, I'd heard stories about the beautiful afterlife. As a reaper, I'd never set a foot bone there. My eternal role took me to the brink of the next world—not a step closer. As long as my services were needed in the in-between, I was happy to oblige and give souls safe passage. I was the critical link between earthly sorrows and the profound bliss of the beyond.

"I didn't want to come back." He shook his head and stared vacantly out into the murky water. A mild wind blew over the frigid river, tugging the top layer of the water and creating small waves. The tiny waves pushed and pulled, making my old lightweight boat slightly unstable.

His eyes grew downcast, and I just wanted to hug the guy.

But I didn't. I maintained my professionalism and kept paddling. A darkness and dreariness surrounded the river as far as the eye could see. An atmospheric fog hung over the equally dark, bottomless water. The drabness was the polar opposite of that illustrious warm light I'd heard about on the other side.

"I reunited with my dog, who'd died a long time ago," my client said, his eyes filling with tears. "Whiskers came running from a bush in a pretty flower garden and leaped into my arms. He licked my face and wagged his tail like he was excited to see me."

I offered him a tissue. He accepted it and dabbed his eyes.

"Out of nowhere, my grandparents ambled over and showered me with hugs and kisses." He looked up at me, his eyes glistening. "Reaper, you just don't know how much that meant to me."

"No, I don't," I admitted. I prided myself on my frankness. But I offered a little compassion whenever I could. Traveling from one world to the next was never easy. It was like trying to reach Mongolia's Gobi Desert, via its hard bumpy roads, no water or electricity to ease the sojourn, and being worryingly isolated. But once a traveler reached the vast scenic landscape, with its richly hued sandy dunes, towering cliffs, and the occasional pair of

Bactrian camels, it made the excruciating trip worth all the effort. I took a cue and made it my mission to ensure my clients journeyed as comfortably as possible.

"As I settled into the afterlife, believing I'd bathe forever in its love and the brightest light I'd ever seen, I was told there'd been some mistake. I had to return to life." His voice trailed as he wrapped his arms around his knees and lowered his chin between them. "I resisted."

"Who wouldn't?" I asked. "But here you are."

The brink of Earth grew increasingly more visible as we approached through the misty water. My client sobbed, hunched over and biting his lip. Again, I offered the last of my tissues. I kept a supply on hand, just in case souls needed to express their angst about leaving life so soon. But rarely did I need to console a client who'd had to be returned and lamented his fate. In fact, never in seven hundred years did I need to bring back a soul so they could hop back into their bodies. It had me stumped too.

But I was merely a staff-level employee. I had no say in whether a soul stayed or went, even if they cried bitterly in my boat. I took my orders and performed my duties with, if I might add, uncommon exactness. I made every effort to see to it that clients were transported per the schedule, which meant double-checking it to maintain accuracy with every pickup. Under my watch, never did an unfortunate soul hang in dreary limbo.

Nevertheless, it was unheard of that anyone be returned. Once a soul reached the periphery of the next world, they stayed for eternity. It was a done deal.

We arrived at the Earthly boundary. I extended my arm bone, and, shaking, my client took it, using it to balance himself as he stepped off the boat.

He gave me one last mournful look, tears flooding his eyes.

"Don't worry. We'll meet again. Hopefully, it'll be at the right time," I said, flashing my set of pearly whites.

He trudged into the distance, his head hung low and all the color drained from his face. With an audible whoosh, he merged with his injured body and, in the blink of an eye, was back to the land of the living.

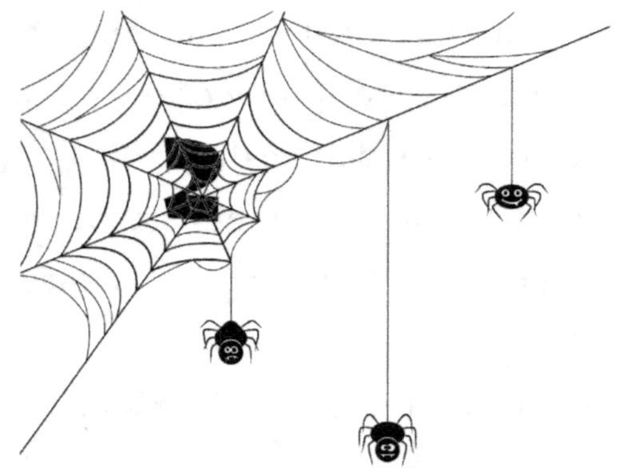

I had barely delivered three more souls before I received another text from Moe.

I pulled out my phone and read his message. I banged my hand bone against my forehead bone. It hurt a little. Still, the spirit guide had asked me to return two more souls.

What in the afterworld was going on?

Huffing and puffing, I paddled my boat across the river back to the brink of eternity. My posture stayed rigid, curses dropping from my agape jawbone as I rowed.

Moe stood on the banks with half-lidded gray eyes, clutching the delicate arms of two shivering female souls on either side of him.

The riverbank melded with the edge of eternity. The chill of the river drifted partially over the banks of the glorious, comfortable, and perfectly temperate afterlife—

which explained the reason the two souls were shivering. Beyond their trembling bodies, their eyes appeared listless. Granted, Moe's tight grip on their slender arms didn't lend much comfort.

I approached the periphery with an impatient sneer. "What gives, Moe? This is the second time I've been asked to return souls."

The spirit guide shook his head, his dirty gray beard wiggling. With his wandering gaze, he appeared zoned out, not making an effort to show the least bit of empathy. Maybe he, too, was preoccupied with the dilemma of all these souls being returned. "I don't know, Reaper. But they need to go back."

"I can't take them both at the same time." I flipped my hand bone, dismissing his implication.

"It'll save time," Moe said, trying to convince me to get rid of them fast. He pushed one of them forward.

She stumbled a couple feet into the shallow part of the water. I leaped off my boat and, with the bottom of my midnight cloak dragging in the river, offered her my hand bone.

"Nope," I assured the spirit guide. "The reaper doesn't do rideshare services."

As much as it would have saved me a second trip back to the edge of the afterlife, I practiced professional integrity. Each soul, whether they headed toward eternity or, in this case, back to the land of the living, deserved a one-of-a-kind trip. I mean, my clients didn't die every day and deserved a special experience when they did. I was committed to giving my undivided attention to the sole passenger in my boat. If they shivered, I offered a cozy blanket. If they wanted to chat, our genuine conversations would be held confidential. These niceties weren't possible while transporting two unacquainted souls, like they were strangers sharing a taxi.

"I never thought I'd see you again," the soul said as she took my hand bone and stepped one foot onto the boat, stopping mid-stride to proclaim her justified amazement.

"Eh, same here," I replied, escorting her nimble body in.

Moe waited with the other soul on the banks as I floated my boat in the opposite direction. His free arm hung limply at his side. A spirit guide of few words, he didn't bother to talk to the soul on his arm and ignored her even as she grimaced, likely in utter confusion at the whole afterlife fiasco.

My return client closed her eyes, as if luxuriating in the sensation of the cool river breeze against her cherub-like face. With a calm expression and her chin lifted, she looked to be a fearless one.

"You know, Reaper," she said in an even tone. "Being on the other side was more animated than I imagined."

"How's that?" My oar probed the serene water. The boat, cozy enough for two, glided gently through it.

"Once I stepped into the afterlife, a thousand screens lit up around me." Her mouth dropped open, and her fingers touched her parted lips.

"Like televisions?"

"Just like televisions," she said, doing a double take. "On each screen, I saw an event from my life replay." She fanned out her fingers, pressing them against her chest.

"Huh, uncanny."

"It was wild. I didn't know the afterlife used technology."

"Me neither. Eh, lots of things are surprising there."

As I continued plunging my oar into the river, we talked about how the events of her life played back on the screens, her accomplishments, and the things she wished she'd done differently.

"Maybe you'll get another chance," I offered. "Going back and all."

"Maybe," she said with a smile. "Thanks, Reaper. That was cathartic."

"No problem. We'll be doing it again sometime. See you soon."

She stepped off my boat and, with a pep in her step, sauntered back into the realm of the living.

I let out a long exhale, brought out my phone, and checked my schedule. A client waited to be picked up in Nepal, and here I was still on the river. Moe and the second returning soul were also expecting me.

I jerked my skull back and took in a sharp breath. *How was I going to manage this?*

Growing uneasy, I rubbed my nasal bone. Maybe if I hurried, I could return the soul to the earthly sphere, then rush to Nepal to give the awaiting soul safe passage.

It was a plan—the only one I could come up with on the spot.

Making haste, I paddled as fast as I could over the river and back to the edge of eternity.

Moe waited motionless, his dull gray eyes gazing blankly out. The soul on his arm appeared bored out of her mind. I couldn't leave my clients waiting. I leaned forward, as if that would force my boat to travel faster through the water. I'd seen it before. Figureheads carved onto the bows of ships sailing speedily over the rough waves, promising calm amid agonizing tumult. My situation took the cake for being tumultuous, as my services were demanded in two places at once.

I reached out my arm bone before my boat hit the sandbar, my skeletal frame unbalanced and nearly toppling into the water. A wet reaper wasn't a happy reaper, especially considering the water was ice-cold and I didn't fancy paddling half-drenched amid the chill looming over the river.

Moe shoved the soul toward me. Saying nothing more and with a glazed-over look, he lumbered back to his post in eternity.

Cautiously, she set one foot into the boat, then another.

I stared at her, secretly fuming. She took her own sweet time, while I didn't have that luxury. I crossed my arm bones over my rib cage and scowled.

Finally, she made herself comfortable at the far end of the boat. I narrowed my eye sockets and paddled swiftly, intensely focused on arriving at the earthly shore.

Doubling my woes, this return client wasn't a cheery one like the last.

"Reaper," she said with a snort. "Did you know that, in the afterlife, they had the nerve to sit me down and judge me?" Her jaw tightened, and her eyes squinted.

"No, really?"

"Yeah. As soon as I entered the next world, they led me into a stark white room with one chair in the center surrounded by six more." She blew out her breath, rattling her lips.

"At least they gave you a chair."

"Humph. Then they proceeded to show me what I did wrong in life." An exaggerated eye roll followed.

"Sounds awful."

"It was because I'd done a lot of wrongs."

"Shocking."

With a seemingly permanent ugly twist of her mouth, she continued to complain during the entire course of the journey. Once we reached our destination and she exited to the earthly realm, I wiped by browbone and sighed in relief. Some souls just made the trip to the other side seem longer.

I stood with my hand bones on my hip bones. Kind of like Super Reaper.

"Next stop, Nepal."

After being stretched to my limits, just the thought of traveling out of my way—in a narrow timeframe—exhausted me. Making matters worse, the prior soul's constant whining had zapped my energy.

Conjuring a Herculean effort, I made my way to Asia, where my client sat atop the summit of Mount Everest. He had been a mountain climber, and met his fate at an elevation of 29,032 feet.

I checked my digital watch. *Phew. I'd barely made it on time.*

I whisked his soul away.

Over the next several weeks, my stress intensified. Souls had to be returned nonstop and my usual workload didn't lessen. I was constantly overstimulated, unable to relax as I hustled to and from the edges of the afterlife and the banks of the living.

Even though the afterlife extended into infinity, my time was finite. Only so many souls could be crammed into each shift. And my shifts continued 'round the clock.

My normal workload quadrupled with countless souls having to go back. My stress hormones sped into overdrive, leaving me battling new aches and pains, stabbing sensations in my rib cage, complete exhaustion, and mild dizziness. I didn't sleep a wink and instead laid in bed tossing and turning or staring vacantly at the nubs on the popcorn ceiling.

For the sake of my sanity, returning my workload to manageable levels took priority.

Increasingly frustrated, I had to find answers.

Why were all these souls being returned?

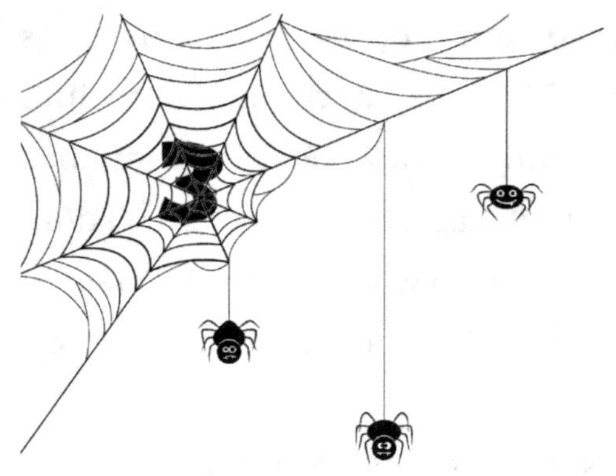

In my limited break time, I made my way to the boss's office.

Clearly, the folks up there in the afterlife didn't know what they were doing, sending souls back to life willy nilly like it was no big deal. Being returned was portentous! Not only to the poor, unwitting souls who'd finally broken free of the earthly chains but to *me*, who had to traverse the cosmic void to see to it that each soul received their eternal reward. Plus, it seemed reasonable that once you were dead, you were dead. Souls didn't have nine lives to squander. Last time I checked, my clients had only one.

Top-level executives, like the Cosmic Light, should've known what they were doing. If even they didn't, who in the next world could us lesser folks believe? Surely the eternal advisory board must've expressed some concern to the Cosmic Light, the bigwig overseeing the whole afterlife enterprise.

I certainly had professional concerns. The past few weeks had overwhelmed me. I'd crushed one too many empty soda cans against my forehead bone. My naturally grim expression had turned even grimmer. I'd demanded perfection in my role before, but now my perfectionist streak was beyond reason. I dreaded my sonic alert skull alarm clock going off each morning, and I no longer possessed the drive to pick up clients with all the confusing shenanigans the afterlife had been pulling. In fact, I felt totally alone in the world—and the afterworld.

A reaper who felt helpless couldn't possibly perform with stellar exactitude. But failure was the downward direction I'd been heading toward lately. If I didn't cure my burnout, I'd find myself slacking—and soon, without a career. No reaper wanted to be banished into the emptiness of oblivion.

I arrived at the office, which was eerily quiet. Bubbly Life—Death's constant companion—chatted up the staff. One of her many fine qualities that secretly enamored me to her. Despite her high rank, she wasn't below swapping dinner recipes or inquiring about our weekend hobbies. But not today.

Cautiously, I tiptoed to Death's door.

It stood ajar. Luckily, the boss was in the office. He usually cracked the door open whenever he was in. He was an open-minded guy, always ready to hear employees' suggestions about how to make the dying process a little less standoffish, and a lot more appealing. An untimely end, he figured, deserved as much celebration as an anticipated beginning.

Arms swinging and my rib cage thrust out, I neared his door. The golden glow of sunlight shone through his floor-to-ceiling window. All I had to do was ask a few pointed questions and this whole issue would be resolved straight away—I hoped. The afterworld would lighten its weight on my shoulders, and my workload would be back on track.

With a lightheartedness gushing through my bones, I poked my skull through the partially open door.

"Hey, boss?"

He didn't reply. The side of his head rested flat on his massive oak desk. Death must've been asleep.

"Oh, sorry. I didn't mean to bother you," I said, and quickly popped my skull back out.

Hmm. Death must've had a long night, napping like a babe at the start of the workday. I shrugged my shoulder bones. Every being who went to sleep eventually woke up—unless they were dead. Being an integral part of the eternal web of existence, Death never died.

So I waited, mindlessly fumbling with random papers on my desk, then grabbing a bag of organic corn chips and an orange juice box from the break room. Coming to the office had its perks, like free crunchy snacks, which gave a weary reaper like me a welcome mid-morning energy boost.

In the meantime, I checked my list, only to see my services were in demand. I left the office briefly to pick up and return a couple more souls before rushing back to speak to the boss.

It'd been a couple hours, so Death certainly had to be awake by now. I plodded back to the office and across the cold white tile floor, which sent a chill up my bare feet bones. I traversed the thinly carpeted area clustered with offices and cubicles. This time, I knocked on the boss's door. Maybe several loud thuds of my hand bone against the wooden door would give him a jolt.

"Boss?" I peeked through the door.

Dagnabbit! He was still asleep.

My gaze darted. I dragged my finger bones down my cheekbones, then pushed the door open. The bright light from the window illuminated his desk—littered with bottles.

Hmm?

I took a step closer.

The bottles lay on their sides—not a drop left in them.

I halted mid-step, tilting my skull and lifting a brow bone.

These were no ordinary bottles. They were empty bottles of high-proof spirits. No wonder the overpowering whiff of alcohol whacked me in the nasal bones like a jackhammer.

Tingling, I moseyed over and picked up a tall, clear bottle with a red ring around its neck. "192 proof," the label said. Death had been drinking Polish-made vodka—on the job.

My eye sockets widened.

Next to the bottle of vodka lay a frosted bottle, also empty. I examined the label—it was a high-proof single malt. Whiskey. Strong enough to power a race car.

I licked my mandible at the sight of this treasure trove of liquor. Staring out the window, I imagined savoring a gut-punching drink right now. A rich, smooth whiskey burning down my throat bones to center me and lift my mood. I fancied a good bottle of whiskey or vodka any day, almost every day. But I took pride in my professionalism and never drank at work.

A kick of my foot bone sent a tall, slender bottle rolling across the floor. I looked down and picked up the empty bottle. "Absinthe."

I took two steps back.

Death had a penchant for powerful drink, but I didn't realize he had a stomach this strong.

Empty bottles of rum and bourbon whiskey sat at the top of the file cabinet, at the edge of his desk cluttered with loose-leaf papers, and even in the dry soil of the wilting Kentia palm in the corner.

Everywhere I looked, empty liquor bottles filled the office.

I stood speechless.

To my knowledge, Death had never passed out from drinking. If he did at home, that was his business. But drinking on the job came with serious consequences. I covered my jawbone. My skeleton tensed up. I had a mind to get to the bottom of this unusual predicament. So I snooped around.

I lifted a premium bottle of rum and held it up to the cascading light. "Humph, the boss has fine taste in liquor." If he wasn't my superior, we might've been drinking buddies.

Under the bottle lay a sheet of paper with a dried brown circular rum stain.

Holding it close to my eye sockets, I inspected the paper. Death's process for scheduling passings began with him handwriting them on paper, then entering them on a spreadsheet on his computer. He texted me the list of souls as an attachment. This was the new, contemporary way of doing business, far less clunky than me juggling paper lists all day and night as I did my rounds.

"Hmm, the numbers seem fine," I said, scrutinizing the handwritten dates.

Death's computer was still on. I leaned over his head and examined the data on the screen. "Here...the dates seem off."

Comparing the numbers on the paper to the numbers on the screen offered a captivating clue.

I homed in on the digits, compelled to investigate the discrepancies.

My skeleton perked up.

Instead of the year 2036, Death had typed in 2026. His finger must've slipped in his drunkenness, causing him to mistype the year of death.

I leaned forward, scanning the papers from top to bottom and checking the computer. My brow bones furrowed and released. My breath hitched.

Most of the dates of death had been mistakenly entered years *too soon*. No wonder the spirit guide kept sending souls back.

Death had been making grave mistakes!

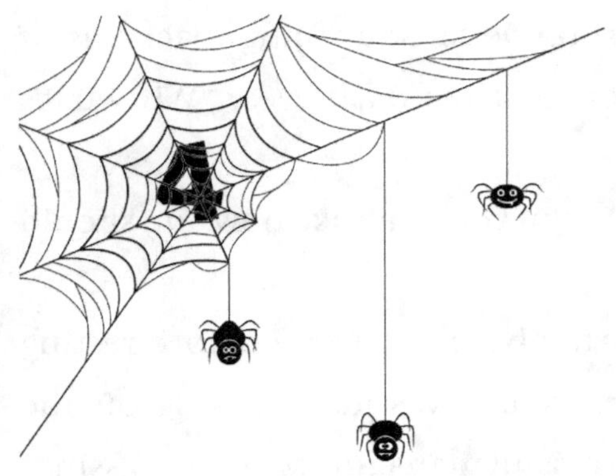

I looked at him sideways and winced. What a pitiful sight, seeing someone as intimidating, powerful, and everlasting as Death in a drunken spiral. Just goes to show that one of the world's two most formidable forces—the other being Life—commanding the world could crumple and be temporarily out of commission as readily as a broken stoplight on the road of life.

It was in the boss's best interests—and mine—to wake him up.

"Death!" I shouted in his ear. "Boss, can you hear me? It's Reaper."

He didn't rouse or twitch a muscle.

I curled my puny finger bones over his burly shoulders, strapping as a quarterback's, and shook him.

He didn't stir.

Then I pinched his dangling earlobe—hard.

Death rolled his shoulders, squirming back, as if writhing in pain. He opened his dark eyes. "Wh-what's happening?"

"Boss, you passed out. But you're awake now and should be fine."

"I did?" His eyes darted here and there before resting on the bottles. "He-he, well, I was just sleeping off the liquor. You know how stressful managing so many passings can be. A few drinks are a lifesaver."

I narrowed my eye sockets. "Mm-hmm."

He scratched his sallow cheek, looking a little dazed.

"Well," I started, clearing my throat and standing alert. "I've got a few souls to pick up. Rather, I've got a lot of souls to collect. Actually, way too many souls. In fact, I'm being bombarded by souls."

Death didn't seem to take the hint. It obviously wasn't a good time to bring up his drinking on the job, and the taxing effect it was having on my workload. Maybe once he sobered up, he'd be more clear-headed and open to acknowledging his serious professional mistakes.

"I'll check in later." Off I went to perform my rounds and returns.

As I journeyed across the cosmos toward Siberia, it occurred to me that Death had made errors in prior centuries too—but never at this magnitude. I remembered returning a handful of souls every hundred years or so. It hadn't been their time either. Occasional slipups were natural, even expected when jillions of permanent exits occurred every second. After all, Death wasn't on the same level of genius as the Cosmic Light, the creator of all beings, including the brilliant progenitor of both Death and Life.

The boss had flaws, like the rest of us immortals. Still, I couldn't help but to seethe at the strain his screw-ups had now put on my once-satisfying, relatively unblemished career.

I arrived at the apartment in Yakutsk, where my client awaited me. His frozen body sat on an old wooden chair covered in icicles, which hung clear and blue and sharp—sharp enough to give me another client if they, by chance, fell. Even my skeleton shivered in the minus fifty-degree temperature. My client's heating had failed, and he'd frozen to death. The entire city, blanketed in ice and snow and whiplashed with subfreezing temperatures, felt like one mega-size freezer.

Despite the savage conditions, the soul greeted me with a smile. "Reaper, am I glad to be out of that stone-cold body. It's far warmer as a soul. I like it much better." He still had his arms wrapped around himself, as if out of habit to keep himself warm.

"Wait until you reach the afterlife," I said, "where it's a balmy seventy degrees all eternity long. You'll like it even better."

With a rapid nod of his head, a gleam in his eye, and his double insulated slip-on boots pointing forward, he climbed into my boat.

My client sat quiet, as if indulging in the serenity and ease of being a new soul, while we traversed the length of the river. This soul was one I particularly hoped would not have to go back. He'd already suffered a terrible death, his once-warm body having been frozen alive. Even a reaper felt sympathy and didn't want an innocent client to endure a repeat of the harshness of life in some Arctic no man's land.

As soon as the soul stepped one foot onto the banks of eternity, Moe pushed forward another soul.

"This one needs to go back," he said gruffly, his lips pursed and his gray eyes squinting. Clearly, he, too, had grown tired of the constant back and forth. Death had really messed up.

"Ugh, fine." My stance grew stiff, and my hand bones locked into fists. I felt sudden pain in my jaw. I was in no mood to return the soul to the living after having just delivered one.

The return client, a wiry redhead of about thirty and dressed in a garish yellow skirt that hurt my eye sockets, stepped onto the boat. I didn't possess the will to help her aboard, even as the boat rocked in the water. She stumbled a bit before getting her footing and settling at the opposite end.

All I needed was a little peace and quiet to deliver the soul without any fuss, then be on my way.

But she opened her mouth and started yapping.

With a grunt, I placed one hand bone over my empty eye socket and slid it down my face bones.

"You know, the coffee is amazing in the afterworld," she said.

"Yeah, so I hear," I replied, humoring her. "Most things are over there."

"As a coffeeholic, I feel a little bitter."

Another whiner. My empty insides roiled as I held my elbow bone tightly against my rib cage. "Why's that?" I asked in a monotone voice, keeping my end of the conversation brief.

"The coffee in the earthly sphere is terrible in comparison."

She let her inhibitions go as she complained for the entire duration of the trip about how awful earthly coffee tasted. She discussed the poor quality of water used in every cup, the staleness of beans, the bad roasting. She went on to say the beans were often ground too coarsely, and, at other times, too fine.

"And now I have to drink subpar coffee for the rest of my days. How unfair! Eternity was like a limited-time special.

Why give me a taste of heavenly coffee then immediately take it back, forcing me to settle for less?"

Little Miss Sunshine crossed her arms and huffed.

In her irksomeness, she stomped her foot against the bottom of my boat, my fragile, age-old boat.

And I lost it.

"Now you listen here, missy," I snapped. "My boat is *not* a stomping ground for your fury. If you don't like earthly coffee, then don't drink it. Wait until your final moment has come to take your grand sip of premium eternal coffee."

I plunged the oar through the water's surface with unusual force.

The splash sent water flying, much of which drenched her red hair. Dripping wet, she flung her neck back and parted her lips. Her eyes looked glassy, as if flooded by tears that had not yet fallen.

She said nothing the rest of the way. I let her off at earth's edges.

Granted, I didn't mean to blow my top. But the accumulating stress of all these returns had its way with me. Helpless, I broke.

"Try Costa Rica," I called after her. "I hear they have good coffee."

Without a word, she disappeared back into the land of the living.

Several pickups and returns later, I arrived at headquarters. I'd grown keenly aware that my returns hadn't been going well. Too many returns accompanied by infuriating tantrums. I could no longer bear the constant whining. Rarely did a soul want to go back to Earth after getting the scintillating, ambrosia-like taste of the afterlife. And I took the brunt of their rage.

With a droopy skeleton, I stumbled into the building.

Right away, Death called me, in no soft tones, into his office.

"Yeah, boss?" I sniveled.

"Reaper, I've received some complaints about you," he thundered, his dark eyes glowering at me from under his narrowing bushy eyebrows.

"Oh?" My face bones turned ashen. I gulped down a breath.

"Souls have been complaining to Moe that your customer service is lacking."

"Well, see, boss, I've been a little swamped lately and—"

"No excuses, Reaper. We run a popular enterprise. Souls think highly of the afterlife. And you need to provide a first-class experience of getting them there. Your unprofessional attitude isn't tolerated. Customer service is a priority here. One more time, and you'll be looking for another eternal position."

I slumped my shoulder bones. All my problems were because of Death's mistakes, and he didn't even realize it.

His words were slurred, as he harangued me about the importance of customer service: the need to improve soul retention rates—as if anyone wanted to leave the afterworld once they got there—how happy souls always gave referrals, the reasons eternity relied on an enhanced brand reputation, and the need to project an inviting image of the great beyond. Yak, yak, yak.

Every time he opened his mouth, my nasal cavity inhaled the pungent smell of vodka.

Death was drunk again, and boy was he a mean one.

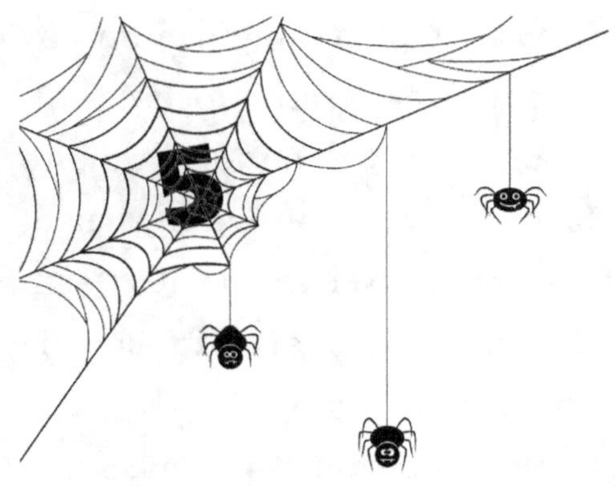

I was determined to get to the bottom of Death's sudden heavy reliance on liquor. My job and my sanity remained precariously on the line, prolonging my unending professional woes. An unhappy reaper was a counterproductively grim reaper. Whatever led the boss to drink excessively—to the point of no return—had to be rectified, and pronto.

A few days later, after frantically shooting to and from the earthly bank to eternity's edge, I took a breather back at headquarters. As an overtasked reaper, there was nothing like feeling anchored, and the office provided that brief sense of comfort.

Death's door was ajar, which meant he was in. I strolled past, noisily crunching on a bag of garden veggie chips from the break room, and shot a glance inside.

The boss sat upright, busily typing away like on any ordinary workday. He seemed alert and focused—his normal qualities. In his sobriety, it was an ideal time to bring up workplace problems. Once I finished my bag of chips, I'd walk over and start my conversation with Death about all these souls being returned and his role in allowing those ongoing fiascos to continue.

He'd patiently listen to my professional grievances and make amends. He always did. Death was the ideal boss: caring, transparent, and reasonable enough to take quick, decisive action to make work easier on the staff. He was a champion of conflict resolution too.

I just wondered how well he'd handle those caused by his own careless errors.

I dug my finger bones into the bottom of the foil snack bag 'til I could hear it crinkle, then plucked out a greasy veggie chip. Despite the hype, I doubted veggie chips offered any more health benefits than regular potato chips. Regardless, I munched on them mindlessly, then crumpled up the bag and tossed it into the waste basket like a basketball. It missed its target. I leaned over and put the rumpled bag in its proper place. The office had a no-litter policy, which made working here kind of nice and clean. Management really did care about the health and well-being of staff.

Turning in my swivel chair and wiping the grease off my hand bones on the folds of my cloak, I got up halfway out of my seat, ready to confront Death.

Just then, Life walked toward his office, her fiery red curls bouncing with her every confident step. My nasal cavity inhaled the strawberry-sweet, lingering scent of her hair, fragrant as spring freesia blossoms. At once, my knees turned to Jell-O. Life was the epitome of ravishing beauty, an otherworldly force that had single-handedly created all that lived and breathed. She was responsible for animating the inanimate, infusing joy into a dreary world with her precocious abilities.

I sat there, running my finger bones along the edge of my cloak's neckline, lost in my fantastical daydreams. My gaze turned inward as I smiled wistfully.

How could anyone resist being attracted to her? I certainly couldn't. Life was the warm light of my cold, dark existence, the stunning creature who gave me hope in a hopeless reality. Just looking at her serene, glowing face, with luminous, emerald-green eyes, filled my skeleton with exuberant, spine-tingling delight. Life was one of a kind—nothing like her in the vast, mysterious universe. And here she was, in my presence, just a few feet away. I sighed, a puppy dog in love.

She slammed the office door shut. The loud bang jolted me out of my reverie.

Though Life had closed the door, the sheer force had bounced it partially open. A stream of golden sunlight shone through the crack.

I wasn't sure if she was aware that Death's door wasn't properly closed. But I plonked down, sagging back in the chair. My arm bones hung loosely at my sides. I couldn't bring up my talk with the boss just yet. His partner, Life, kept him busy at the moment.

Life and Death were eternal, steadfast companions. Nothing separated them. Wherever Life was, Death wasn't far behind. It'd been this way since the dawn of existence, which explained why I couldn't be with her as I desired. The couple had been around since time immemorial while, in comparison, I was a rookie. Even my seven hundred years on the job didn't make her look at me any more fondly. I was just a lower-level employee entertaining a mere crush on Life, while the powerful and pervasive Death seized her flighty attention and filled her heart. Life and Death were lost in a whirlwind romance. The situation didn't do me any favors, but how far could a lowly reaper get with such a magnanimous essence?

Without warning, Life's voice escalated to a yell. I heard her every word fall from her full lips.

"Another earthquake? Are you out of your mind?" Life shouted at the top of her lungs. It was more like a guttural roar. I'd never heard her speak so harshly. Still, her voice sounded like a scintillating musical tune, making drastic melodic leaps up and down—a disjunct melody that rose and fell swiftly.

My ear bones perked up. Death mumbled inaudibly.

"And you're going to pair it with a tsunami?" she continued, obviously enraged with all her vocal octave leaps. "Do you know how many people will die in that deadly disaster? Almost 250,000!"

I didn't quite catch how Death replied. Life certainly had sway over him. Even the most powerful masculine force would weaken in the presence of such a stunningly gorgeous entity. It was no wonder he didn't yell back. Life had Death wrapped around her pinky. And he loved it.

"Give me a break!" she shrieked. "I just breathed life into those men, women, and children. Now you're making plans to ruin it all with a tsunami carrying the energy of 25,000 atomic bombs?"

Life's uncontrollable sobs came out loud and clear.

I twisted my neck bone, giving a pained glance toward the door, and tilted my skull to the side.

Poor thing. She might've been in the right. After all, creating life was no minor incident. Life carefully handcrafted every living creature, from the tips of their individual eyelashes to the toenails on their feet, from the tiniest microbes to the largest land mammals on Earth. Living beings were her priceless masterpieces. I couldn't think of one incomplete life form—each were self-contained products of her brilliant machinations, possessing the internal mechanics to function independently.

Death spoke a few words, inaudibly again.

"Don't hug me!" Life screamed and burst out of the office. In a huff, she stomped across the carpeted floor, her hands cupping her wet, tear-streaked face.

My empty chest cavity sank. I sat silently, wanting to ease her angst but not knowing what to say.

She rushed past my cubicle, still radiating sunnily despite her torrential tears. If anyone could look beautiful being so tormented, it was Life.

I slumped in my chair. Maybe now wasn't a good time to bring up all the soul returns with Death.

A weighted feeling overcame my bones. I needed a distraction and fiddled with the paperwork on my desk. I performed a little data entry and created random documents. Reapers had drudge work too.

The wall clock sped forward an hour. A thirst tickled my throat bones. I walked past Death's office to get to the cooler and pour myself a cup of refreshing, chilled water. Being unapologetically nosy, I glanced through the partially open door.

Death had keeled over. His head lay on his outstretched arm over his oak desk.

My brow bones drew together, and I forgot about the water cooler. I poked my face bones farther into his office. My attention zoomed in on his left hand gripping an empty vodka bottle.

He'd passed out again drinking. I rubbed my eye sockets to be sure I was seeing right. Yep, the bottle was clear as crystal, and empty as a clueless stare.

I paused and put two and two together.

Death was struggling with relationship problems with Life, causing him to take to the bottle!

My jawbone fell open. The room became a blur. Time suddenly seemed to slow down. I refused to believe the truth of what I'd just seen but it was impossible to shake the stark reality.

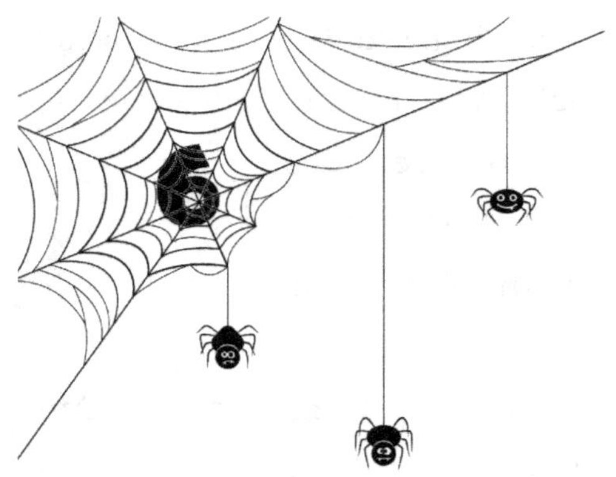

The tsunami hit the Pacific Ocean's Ring of Fire region, pulverizing Chile and the South American coast. Homes, warehouses, and pickup trucks drifted like broken ships in the powerful deluge of muddy debris-filled water. The unstoppable ocean water crept like Hades over the rolling hills and smothered the land. Filthy water, submerging acres upon acres of farmland, steadily flowed at full force, mercilessly blanketing the coastal towns.

Just a day prior, the land had suffered an 8.4 magnitude earthquake. Fires broke out, sending black smoke curling into the sky and casting a sense of menace and doom over everything.

Upon witnessing the vast wreckage, I sighed and slumped my shoulder bones. In a country of nineteen million, over one percent needed my services. Life wouldn't be too happy about this. I could see her now: luscious pink lips pressed tightly in a beautiful grimace while her emerald-green eyes flooded with tears as crystal clear as a serene lake on a summer day.

What I'd give to comfort Life in her time of distress. Maybe wrap my arm bones around her and hold her forever. Nothing in eternity could loosen my grip of her.

Then the sulfurous stench of brown seaweed smacked me in the face bones. I shook my skull clear of my far-stretched reveries and focused my attention on the present dire situation.

Meandering through the towns was nigh impossible. Instead, it took uncommon strength to wade through the scattered knee-high debris, which pierced my feet bones and nicked my leg bones.

I looked ahead at the towering wreckage, a sight my eye attentive sockets couldn't miss. Massive deep ocean steel fishing boats tipped onto their side hundreds of feet away from the harbor, or landed awkwardly in the middle of the downtown streets. Light poles barely clung to the ground as they precariously leaned over, about to topple on unwitting individuals at any second. Six-story buildings had snapped in half like saltine crackers. The few homes left standing had no power or fresh water. Many residences had drifted into neighborhoods five miles away and settled there.

The devastation was too great to stomach, even for an immortal used to working major disasters every few centuries. I covered my eye sockets with my hand bone, intending to pick up my clients blindly.

The Chileans who failed to evacuate were the ones who received a visit from me.

Per custom during large-scale disasters, I began with one soul at a time. My policy was one soul per boat ride. Plus, cutting a monumental task into bite-size pieces usually made the job more manageable. I'd likely be stationed here for a while to collect the quarter-million souls. Swiftness was my forte, however, and I determined to move at a steady pace until the job was done.

I hurried to collect and deliver my clients to their eternal destination. No soul could be left waiting for long. They might begin to doubt that they deserved to enter the gates of the everlasting—and I wanted no such doubts beleaguering their minds. Good customer service was a high priority in the next world.

"Buenas dias!" exclaimed a farmer, his leathery face well-kissed by the Chilean sun, probably for decades. "Como estai?

I exhaled silently. He was the affable sort, the kind I liked having on my boat. They brightened the dreary passage to the next realm.

Having traveled to all parts of the world, I understood his Chilean Spanish and returned his greeting. "Just fine, fine. Not a bad day to make a trip to the afterlife, huh?"

Humoring me with a tolerance only the mature could offer, he offered me a hand-woven basket of cranberries, big ripe ones in colors as deep red as rubies. He'd been loosening the fruits from their vines with the help of eggbeaters, a.k.a. water reels, when the tsunami warning sounded.

"Gracias," I said looking him in his brown eyes. I placed one hand bone on my rib cage while accepting the basket with the other. "It's very kind of you. I'll probably chop them up and make a nice salsa."

"No problemo." With a smile, he confided, "I'd never leave my fields. Nothing gives me greater satisfaction."

He gave his life for his farm. Understanding his admirable commitment, I placed his gift at my end of the boat. With slow easy breaths, I rowed him across the river.

After the pleasant drop-off on the banks of eternity, I was about to return to the site of the natural disaster when Moe came running out from the low-drifting fog.

"Reaper, wait!" he screamed, waving his arms frantically. As he ran, he pulled along a pale soul by the arm. His fingers clutched the soul so tightly that they turned white.

"What now?" I asked, clenching my teeth. "I've got a bunch of souls waiting for me. Death's unleashed another tsunami."

Moe puttered. "Well, this one needs to go back." The spirit guide shoved the hapless soul forward.

I thought customer service was a big deal in the afterworld. How come no one ever complained about Moe's callous treatment of return souls?

Never minding the answer, as 249,999 more clients were pending, I brought the soul onboard. A tightness grew in my rib cage as I anticipated a deluge of upcoming return souls, coupled with the inordinate number of souls already on the Chilean coast. The spike in my workload demanded gargantuan effort on my part, making my brow bones furrow.

Drawing my breath, I released it gradually. I'd heard diaphragm breathing eased stress.

"So what's your story?" I asked, paddling with a stiff skeletal posture. My conscious breathing failed to deliver the effect I'd assumed it would.

"Um, I'm not sure. As soon as I arrived, they asked each other what I was doing there," he replied with a dramatic Italian shoulder shrug. "They said since I was already there, I might as well get a tour."

"Oh, a tour of eternity. How was it?" I hadn't heard this one before.

He stretched out his long legs in the boat and gestured wide with his arms. "Spotless white buildings held up by Grecian pillars. Clean floors. Not a dust particle in sight. I'd definitely go back."

Ah, the neat freak didn't have much of a choice. Souls, no matter how idiosyncratic, ended up in the afterworld, sparkly clean or not.

In a short time, we arrived back to the earthly banks. He hopped off the boat. My sense of empathy fading, I returned to the site of the tsunami.

In that chaotic aftermath, I robotically performed my gruesome duties. Soon, my mind began drifting to a more palatable scenario. Something pleasing, inspiring, undeniably beautiful.

Life.

I took a deep, cleansing breath and smiled wistfully, even as I picked up souls hovering patiently above the mountainous piles of rubble.

The lovely creature found herself in a mess, not wanting this deadly tsunami in the first place. Yet Death had ignored her pleas and pushed onward with his plans. I scratched my skull. Why would he do such an insensitive thing? The boss had always been mysterious, taking random lives as soon as they let out their first cry while leaving others to endure misery for eighty or ninety years.

Now he was giving Life grief—with nobody there to console her.

My empty chest cavity grew heavy.

No one left my eternal crush in tears. If Death didn't comfort her, a more compassionate entity would: me. I was a mere step down from the boss. He arranged for deaths while I escorted souls to their eternal resting place. We were both closely involved in the flourishing business of death. Considering Life adored Death, she might take a liking to someone similar. So it made perfect sense that I'd be the one to offer Life sympathy, to relieve her of her unbearable woes.

Thrusting out my rib cage, I lifted my chin bone high. Death wasn't in a position to be the man—but I was. At once, I felt ten feet tall.

I'd be the bag of bones Life could rest her pretty little head on, the fierce dark knight clamoring to save his languishing princess. The frightful phantasm who'd distract her from her sadness and replace it with a rush of giddy happiness.

She'd fall for me. Maybe Life would even give up her attachment to Death. Could Life exist without Death and vice versa? It'd never before happened in the history of the world. Even glass sponges, the rare marine life with a 15,000-year lifespan, eventually succumbed to the hands of Death.

I curled my finger bones, rubbed them against my cloak, and blew on them. As the grim reaper, I had plenty of experience comforting souls when I gave them safe passage to the other side. Offering solace wasn't part of my job description; I simply did it to elevate the singular experience of transitioning from life to eternal peace and bliss. Call me ambitious, but I went above and beyond my formal duties.

And I intended to do the same for Life. She meant the afterworld to me.

In the thick of the other hundreds of thousands of souls awaiting me, I conjured up a hand bone full of ideas to comfort irresistible Life.

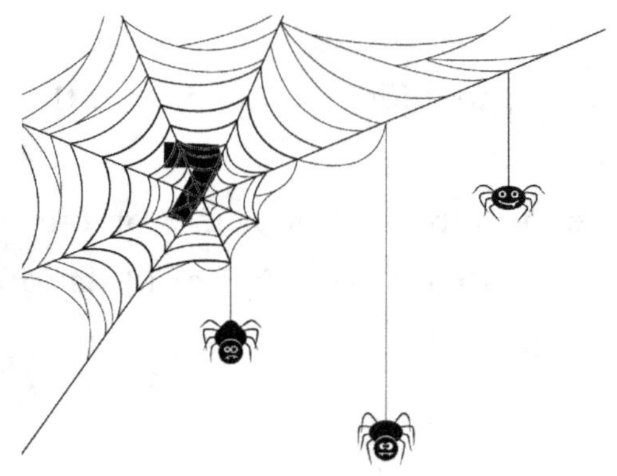

7

My schedule grew busy in the aftermath of the Chilean tsunami. Although that exhausting ordeal was finally over, I still worked at odd hours, put in significant overtime, and collected more clients than usual with the onslaught of ridiculous soul returns.

There simply weren't enough hours in the day, as the list of return souls kept growing. Death must still have been drinking heavily and making careless errors in the scheduling—a clear sign that Life and Death continued their relationship-straining disagreements. "Fights" was a more accurate term: brawls, flat-out clashes between the two mightiest forces known in the earthly sphere.

My chances at gaining Life's favor grew exponentially with every fallout. I was by no means an opportunist; rather, I saw myself as a romantic visionary, jumping at the chance to hold her in my arm bones, push her fiery red hair back, and whisper sweet nothings in her ear.

Amid the constant hustle and bustle, I kept to what was most important: ravishing Life. I'd squeeze in time for my everlasting crush no matter what it took or how many gazillion miles I had to traverse the cosmos to comfort her. I could come up with endless praises, from her vivacious personality to her special way of making me feel like the only one in existence. Sincere compliments, random acts of kindness, and my undivided attention ought to uplift her. After centuries of working in the same office, certainly I could speak her love language and be the support and understanding she needed.

She must've felt awfully deceived and rejected by Death, her constant companion, as he refused to consider her feelings when making his catastrophic decision. But I'd let her know her distress and anger were valid emotional responses to the heartbreaking natural disaster he'd unleashed with little restraint.

One day at the office, shortly after the Chilean tsunami, I ran into Life. She carried a handful of papers in her fair arms, smooth as silk.

As I looked sideways, fiddling with my scythe, my lanky skeleton bumped into her eternal body.

"Oh, excuse me, Reaper," she said apologetically, dropping her papers. "I didn't mean to bump into you."

"No, no. Excuse *me*," I blurted out. "I should've seen you coming." A flush crept across my cheekbones. I began swallowing excessively, the back of my neck bones all atingle. Lowering my chin bone, I bent down and picked up the papers that had scattered across the gray low-pile carpet.

I shuffled the papers awkwardly in my hand bones, trying to stack them neatly before handing them back to her. "You look a little sad today," I stammered, hoping she didn't notice me breaking out in a sweat.

"Oh, it's nothing. I've got work on my mind. So much goes on behind the scenes in the world of the living." She grasped the papers against her chest, her arms hugging herself as if in an act of self-soothing.

"Yeah, it sure does." I paused for a moment then seized my chance. "How 'bout some fresh air? It'll do you good, reinvigorate you. I'll bet you'll be all smiles afterward."

As she faced me, her doleful green eyes penetrated my soul. I quivered. No longer did I notice the cubicles to the left, the management offices beyond them, or the copy machine in the far corner of the office. Life, in her scintillating glory, received every last drop of my attention.

The ends of her pouty lips curled upward. She exhaled, as if letting out eons of disappointment. In a voice as soft as a down pillow, she replied, "That'd be nice, Reaper."

I beamed.

She held out her elbow, and I took it. With a bounce in my step, I sauntered out of the building with her by my side and entered the office park area lined with blooming trees and manicured hedges. The air was clean and crisp, the sun at just the right point in the sky for a pleasant warmth. Its rays seemed to glisten like diamonds on Life's supple skin. I paid little heed to nature's bounty—I was in paradise.

The sidewalk led us up and down gently rolling hills. I glanced over at Life without turning my skull. Her once tight expression had relaxed, as if she'd been calmed by nature's splendor.

This was my once-in-an-existence chance to get closer to Life.

"If you need to vent, I'm all ear bones," I said, as we walked side by side, my arm bones swinging. I was in my element, feeling a completeness I'd never experienced before. Life didn't know it, and neither did anyone else in the scheme of things, but she was secretly my other half. At least I wanted her to be.

"Thank you, Reaper." She didn't speak for a minute, as if carefully pondering her next words. "It's just that the tsunami was so unnecessary."

"I agree. You worked hard crafting those living creatures, from the panicky humans scrambling to evacuate right down to the torn-up Bull Kelp algae floating in the Pacific."

"In the blink of an eye, it was swept away." Life scrunched her face, her angst on clear display.

"Right. Tsunamis are a rare event on Earth. I'd say they occur maybe twice every ten years." Perhaps my brazen show of knowledgeable facts would impress her.

"All the instant damage and final passings. I—" Life seemed to be choking back tears.

Eh, my nuggets of knowledge did no such thing.

"Here." I offered her a tattered end of my draping cloak.

"Uh, thanks, Reaper." She dabbed her eyes with it.

I noticed a bench up ahead. I motioned for her to sit down, and we did.

"You know, I'd love to tell you some skeleton jokes," I said hoping my grin would be contagious.

"Oh, really?" she said, still sniffling.

"Yeah, they're pretty humerus."

She threw her head of fiery red hair back and laughed, her long tresses falling against the back of the wooden bench like a rushing waterfall. Her laughter ricocheted through the park, bouncing off stone walls and livelier than tropical birdsong.

I leaned back with ease and savored my moment of triumph: making Life laugh and ending her woes. At least for now.

A few quiet minutes passed as I rummaged through my skull for more bad jokes. She sighed long and looked out.

"It seems all my efforts are a waste," she cried out, palms raised to her flushed cheeks. "No one knows the degree of hard work that goes into designing, producing, and performing a final quality check of every miscellaneous life form. It takes an enormous amount of physical and emotional energy and discipline to create the miracles of life on Earth."

I couldn't bear to see Life return to being so unhappy. I felt the urge to wrap my arm bones around her robust yet delicate frame. But I resisted, mindful of professional boundaries. My time would come. It just wasn't now.

"I totally get it," I said instead, mirroring her hunched-over posture. "They're your works of art, your masterpieces, your magnum opus. What would Beethoven have done if an aberrant force ripped up his Fifth Symphony in the middle of a concert? Or if a disgruntled entity penciled a mustache on Leonardo da Vinci's Mona Lisa just as the exhibition opened to the public? Your creations are your papooses, your bundles of joy. It's a shame that your little darlings were trampled on such a large scale."

She looked over at me and, with her pink painted lips, smiled genuinely, probably for the first time in days. "I'm glad someone understands. Thanks, Reaper."

My chest cavity nearly burst out of my rib cage.

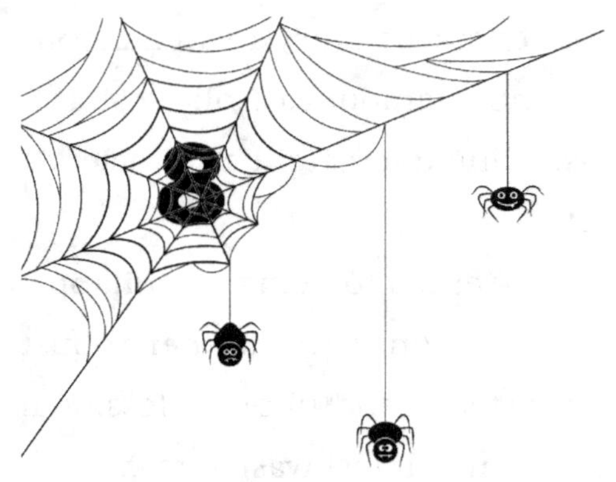

I'd started sipping yerba maté, which I'd discovered in South America during my exhausting rounds after the recent tsunami. The herbal tea gave me smooth and steady energy, which I needed. I preferred the South American native drink to coffee, which only delivered a big, fleeting *oomph*.

The plethora of returned souls compelled me to modify my diet too. I plucked bunches of ripe bananas straight off the trees when my work took me to Central America or Southeast Asia. I stuffed them in my cloak pockets to munch on and preserve my energy levels during strenuous soul collections and returns.

If anything, the onslaught of soul returns forced me to be a healthier reaper.

"Reaper," said one twentyish soul I'd just picked up in Guatemala City. She'd won the Miss Guatemala beauty pageant hours before. She still wore the crown on her head, dotted with shiny blue gems around the bottom rim, and the regal sash that read "Miss Guatemala" in uber-fancy lettering. Her ears dripped with Swarovski crystal chandelier diamond earrings. Her soul sort of sparkled as I rowed through the murky darkness of the river.

"Your complexion is amazing."

"Gee, thanks," I replied, shooting my vertebra up straight.

"What have you been doing for it?" She leaned forward with her hand on her knee. "Tell me your secret, Reaper."

I placed my free hand bone against my rib cage, flattered she wanted to know my facial bone routine. "Oh, it's not much of a secret. I've improved my diet lately, eating more fruits." I laid my finger bone against my cheekbone. "Bananas do wonders for my bone tone."

A relaxed smile crossed her heavily painted face. Clearly, she was pleased to know the beautifying effects of the curvy yellow fruit.

I shared a happy glance with her as we steadily approached the edges of the next realm.

My skull tilted slightly to one side. Unlike many of my clients, this soul was quite the congenial type. No wonder she'd won the famed national pageant. She would've gone far had Death not scheduled her so soon. It took a rare soul to master interpersonal skills and shine on the world stage. She certainly possessed excellent social skills, much needed in the world of pageantry and also highly prized in the afterworld. No one wanted to hang around a grouch for eternity.

I felt slightly pained to let her off on the other side, wishing to exchange more beauty secrets. But duty called, and she had places to be.

Once she stepped off the boat, she turned, flashed a smile, then gave me that stiff, awkward beauty queen wave.

I'm no beauty queen, but I waved back in similar fashion. It wasn't even a wave but more like subtly rotating my hand bone back and forth. The secret to the gesture was in the wrist bone. It struck me that this was how pageant winners and princesses endured long hours of waving during outings and processions and won the public's esteem. With just the right movement, they wouldn't tire of waving. I felt a whoosh of self-confidence, having learned something new.

The amiable pageant winner had been the last soul on my long list for the day. Thank goodness Moe didn't emerge out of the fog with another return. The accumulated tension lifted, leaving me with a rare lightness in my bones.

Free and easy for the time being, I sauntered into the office, noshing on half a banana—my reward for having just finished another heavy workload.

Like a radar, my attention homed in on Life. I intended to catch any energy she reflected. Whatever I couldn't see of my eternal crush, I'd feel.

She sat in her office across from Death's. As I walked past, I slowed my pace, just to get a glimpse of her otherworldly presence. I almost felt the heaviness in her body. Such an incredible phenomenon was expected when two entities connected. She'd lowered her wide eyes, which once glimmered with effervescent joy. Her body posture appeared sunken. And her beautiful round face, like a full moon on a dark night, drooped.

Since the issue of returned souls hadn't yet been resolved, it meant Life and Death were still not on speaking terms.

I sighed, unable to witness this bubbly creature so blue.

Needing to escape the overbearing sadness I detected from her, I did what a concerned reaper would do. I knocked on Life's door. The knock knocks dispelled the sadness like a healer's magic.

She slowly looked up, her large eyes watery and her full lips pouty. "Yes, Reaper?"

"Uh, I just wanted to tell you the souls I've picked up lately absolutely loved their lives." Shifting my feet bones, I dropped my gaze to the floor, unable to suppress my smile. "So, you've done a wonderful job."

"Oh, thanks, Reaper. I try." Her voice, once a vivacious symphony of sounds, came out weak.

I couldn't stand to see her diminished to a paltry entity. I felt the urge to do something. "One of my clients mentioned that the local dog shelter just received a litter of puppies," I said with newfound pep.

Life's green eyes brightened. "Really? I love puppies."

"It shows, given all the adorable qualities you give them. Everyone loves puppies."

"They're among my most favorite creatures to breathe life into," she said, touching her throat.

Inhaling deeply, I mustered up my courage. "If you're up for it, we should visit the shelter and cuddle the pups. It'll take your mind off the gloomier side of work and give you a boost."

She sighed. A small smile appeared from the corners of her lips. She took a minute, as if contemplating my offer.

"I could use a change." She leaped up from her chair and made her way toward me. At once my imagination took me to a green field, where Life ran barefoot through the lush grass, her milky white arms outstretched. I stood waiting at the other end, yearning for her embrace until the end of eternity.

"I'm ready" she said. "Are you?"

I snapped myself out of my daydream. "Um, yeah."

We headed for the dog shelter two miles away. It was a short walk, a mere half hour. But I indulged in every minute of her companionship.

I'd done it again, brought Life by my side. Without Death around, this beautiful force paid me more attention. My hollow core inflated with potent feelings of adoration, I was on the verge of bursting into an operatic song, belting

Figaro's "Non piu andrai" from Mozart's "The Marriage of Figaro."

Taking long strides, I instead chatted with her nonstop. How often did a lowly staff reaper get one-on-one time with the most magnificent presence in the universe?

Today, she'd have the privilege to see another side of me, one outside of the office. If all went well, she'd slowly fall in love with me and desire that we'd be one forever. My empty insides grew giddy.

"Do you know why you shouldn't get into a pillow fight with me?" I asked, intending to lighten her mood. I could pull tons of jokes from up my cloak sleeve. If chose me, she'd be laughing all the time—unlike Death, who left her morose. What did she see in that somber phantasm anyway?

"No, why?"

"It's a bad idea unless you're prepared for the reaper cushions!" I said, capping the punchline with the infamous ba-dum-tss sound.

She clapped, flung her head back, and laughed. "Repercussions!"

She loved even my corniest jokes. What a happy pair we'd make!

I made efforts to contain my uncontainable excitement, which traveled through all 206 bones in my jittery skeleton. A confident reaper was a masculine reaper.

The Infinity Dog Shelter appeared a few yards ahead. I swung open the door for her.

"Thank you, Reaper," she said, and strode in.

I followed her like a puppy dog in love, worshipping her every step.

We exchanged a few words with the volunteers at the front desk and ended up in the puppy kennel.

Life picked up a pup and held her creation in her arms. It was one of six golden retriever pups, with fur as yellow as maize and a spirit as lively as a field of sunflowers. It whimpered, eyes still closed.

"Aww, look at that," I remarked as she cuddled the puppy. "He's right at home in your arms."

Life's smile never left her face as she cradled the animal. "This was a lovely idea, Reaper."

A tingle delighted my bones. I'd done it again, cheering up the light of my existence.

I inched toward Life to stroke the furry pup's wobbly head. As I stood in her intimate space, sensing the warmth of her skin, my chest cavity pulsed. Inches away from the most prolific force in the universe, my joy of togetherness intensified. And I was sure she felt the same.

Death, what a fool! His mistakes only pushed me closer to my eternal love.

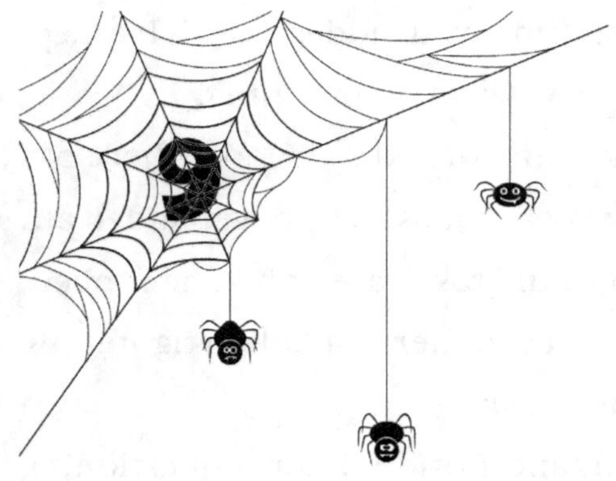

"Ready?" Life asked in a bubbly tone, her striking green eyes meeting my dark, hollow eye sockets. I wanted to drop to my knee bones and sing *Hallelujah*.

"Um, yeah." My voice rose in pitch amid the tingles in my abdominal cavity.

This is the Life I'd always known: upbeat, positive, and fully present in the moment—the way a highly successful vital force should be. How far could Life have gotten if she were perpetually depressed? I didn't mind thinking I had a hand bone in her growing sense of well-being.

We'd scheduled a bit of cycling in the wee hours of the morning before I started my shift. The exercise and fresh air would do her good. As for me, I was on a direct path to everlasting romantic fulfillment. One joyful bike ride was the beginning of many more.

Before starting out, I knelt down and pumped her tires.

"When was the last time you added air?" I asked, attaching the pump to the valve, then pumping.

She shook her thick mane of red hair loose, her soft, shiny curls bouncing like beachballs. "I've never added air. I thought the bike shop would take care of it," she replied, placing a wide brim sun hat over her head, then tightening the wind lanyard until it was snug.

My brow bone lifted, and I offered her a questioning gaze. This was an opportunity to take charge of her tires. She needed someone with brawn to handle her bicycle maintenance. "I'll be here whenever you need them inflated. Just ask."

"Okay."

With the grace of a ballerina, Life hopped on her bike. She dangled her long, slender legs on either side of the bike, sending my hollowness aflutter. A straw basket hung from the bicycle handlebars. Her light blue floral sundress with spaghetti straps revealed her lustrous shoulders, which would in a moment be kissed by the sun. From head to toe, she looked summery—the height of irresistible.

I got on my starter bike, perfect for inexperienced cyclists like me. I teetered and tottered, attempting to gain my balance. I tucked my black cloak neatly away so it wouldn't flap in the wind, get caught in the wheels, and send me flying skull first over the handlebars—which, in the presence of Life, would've turned my ear bones an unabashed red.

I'd suggested cycling through the countryside as a way to ease Life's endless blues. I also knew it released the "feel good" hormones, which was all I needed for Life to associate me with happiness. She still hadn't quite gotten over being snubbed by Death—who should've looked out for his lady.

But he failed, and here I was.

In my mind's eye, I raised my hand bones to the sky, thanking whoever or whatever was responsible.

The ride down the gravely back roads gave us scenic views of the countryside. Fields of purple hyacinths blossomed on either side of us for miles, and the sky was awash with hues of rich baby blues.

"Just look at all the natural beauty you created," I said, between huffs and puffs as pedaling had grown torturous.

"Hmm. Hope no tornado blows it all away," Life uttered dryly.

Gusts of wind blew eastward as we headed westward. The breeze against my cheekbones dispelled all my cares.

Life pedaled effortlessly, turning her neck every now and then to take in the pristine rolling hills, green with pops of purple or yellow flora. She didn't notice me gasping behind her, struggling to keep up. Nevertheless, everything faded away—except the ravishing beauty cycling next to me. I concentrated on the Zen art of cycling, envisioning how I'd extend that rapture to my eternal beloved.

Her countenance appeared tranquil as she leisurely pedaled. She gazed straight ahead with a serene smile. I knew it'd happen: her happy juices had started flowing. She'd associate the feeling of freedom and unbridled joy with her cycling partner, me.

Life's perspective would surely change as we cycled amid breathtaking views and the surge of endorphins. Her worries about Death would disappear, as if his stubbornness and disregard never mattered. It's the little things in eternal existence that counted, little things like a cloaked skeleton who wanted to give his forever crush the afterworld.

"Hey, want to stop at the farmer's market?" I asked, so winded I had to stop pedaling. The idea of a bike ride seemed more practical than actually doing it and succumbing to sheer exhaustion. Maybe I wasn't as fit as I'd thought.

She glanced at the crooked wooden sign on the side of the road.

"Farm fresh vegetables, free range eggs, honey," she said, reading it. "I'd love to!"

We stopped at the colorful stands filled with fresh loaves of French bread, apples just plucked from the orchards, jars of golden honey and strawberry jams, and blueberry muffins baked that morning.

Laying my bike against a tree, I finally got a rest. My nasal cavity picked up the warm, woody scents of cinnamon, and I followed the trail.

Life browsed the baskets overflowing with tasty morsels, picked up mason jars brimming with honey, and chatted with the gregarious farmers. She returned with a long loaf of bread, which she placed in her bicycle basket.

I handed her a bouquet of flowers I'd purchased just for her.

"Aww, thanks, Reaper." She brought the flowers up to her nose and deeply inhaled the rosy fragrance of fuchsia peonies. "Farmer's markets make me feel so connected with the world around me."

Placing my hand bone over my rib cage, I felt so connected with her.

I was sure she felt the same.

In the afternoon, we were scheduled to take banjo lessons. But first, my rounds awaited me.

I collected the flurry of souls on my list and transported them without a hitch to the next realm. As I rowed the final soul to the edge of eternity, I figured I'd be at the banjo lesson with Life in no time. Moe hadn't shown up out of the blue all shift long. I didn't need any return souls to delay my precious moments with Life.

All such hopes were dashed.

As I floated my boat to the banks, Moe appeared out of the dense fog, gripping a writhing soul who looked like he was wrapped in some sort of uncomfortable white contraption.

I'd never seen such a sight before. Though curious, I rowed with hesitation.

Once I reached the shore, the spirit guide explained in gruff tones. "This one's a fighter. Had to restrain him with a straightjacket because he refused to leave."

"Ah." I nodded, understanding his predicament. Not many wanted to leave the eternal realm after being enveloped by the purest form of love ever to be felt. Love in the earthly sphere didn't hold a candle to the genuine blanketing of love known only on the other side.

"Now he's your problem," Moe grumbled, before shoving the soul toward my boat.

The unfortunate soul stumbled and, since his arms couldn't give him balance, fell face-first into the frigid water.

Poor soul had already been rejected by eternity, then restrained in a straightjacket. He needed no further discomfort. I scrambled to pick him up and escort him toward my boat. As I crouched to assist the hapless soul, I turned to Moe to have a firm word with him about customer service. But the spirit guide had already disappeared into the fog.

Cursing under my breath, I led the drenched soul onto the dry boat.

He sat glum the entire journey. Once we reached the earthly shore, I undid the straightjacket, and his arms hung free. But he resisted getting off the boat.

"I don't wanna go back," he said, crossing his arms over his chest. "Make me!"

With my hand bones on my hip bones, I stood stiff as a board. The unruly soul tested my patience. My three o'clock date with Life was fast approaching, and this stubborn client refused to leave.

He scowled like a brute, but that didn't dissuade me. I shouted that he wasn't going back.

His nostrils flaring, he began rocking my boat, like a toddler red in the face and having a tantrum. I nearly lost my balance and fell into the river.

I flipped my lid.

"Listen, mister," I said sternly. "You can stay on the frigid river, or you can do the rest of your time on Earth. But you can't stay in my boat. I've got a hot date and more clients to pick up. Make your choice."

Arms still crossed, he turned his chin.

My leg bones planted wide, I glared at him and cracked my knuckles.

Taking the hint, he plodded off the boat and whooshed back into his mangled body at the scene of his devastating car accident that had sent him to me in the first place.

I sighed with relief.

The banjo lesson was nothing short of fun. Life and I learned to play a five-string banjo.

As she strummed the instrument, she giggled. I hadn't seen her this joyful since her fallout with Death. It was because of me.

After all the fun times we'd spent together lately, I could see she trusted me. We communicated openly and shared a lot of the same interests. Most importantly, Life smiled more, and I could tell she felt supported.

My romantic future held exciting promise.

Tomorrow, we had reservations at a five-star restaurant. In the dim candlelight, I'd express my true feelings for her. She'd reciprocate, leave Death for good, and give her heart to me forever.

I bounced on my toe bones.

Friday night couldn't come soon enough.

The La Next World restaurant smelled of delectable prime steak. The aromas of butter, garlic, and sprigs of rosemary wafted into my nasal cavity, as I followed the scent trail to our table with Life. The *pop pop* sounds of the meat sizzling in the back kitchen lent a spiritedness to the intimate atmosphere.

The dapper waiter, dressed in black slacks, a crisp white dress shirt, and a black bowtie, seated us in a dimly lit corner. I'd specifically requested their most private table beforehand. I had some pretty heavy topics to discuss with the universe's most illustrious femme fatale. The waiter was responsible for our table only, ensuring his special level of attention enhanced our dining experience. I'd dug into my shallow cloak pockets and paid extra for it.

Life plopped down into the vintage French leather dining chair I'd pulled out for her. I scurried over to my seat at the opposite side. Sitting across from this ravishing eternal beauty gave me the once-in-an-existence opportunity to gaze into her dazzling eyes—to pour out my true feelings.

"Why don't we start?" she asked, flipping open her menu.

"I'm down. What'll it be?" I didn't bother to open mine. I was too busy looking at her face, my jawbone ajar. Nothing in the restaurant could distract me from my one-on-one time with Life. I tuned out the soft classical music playing the background, despite it creating a timeless experience for me and my date, and the appetizing aromas that made me salivate like a puppy.

"The pappardelle Bolognese sounds delish," she piped up.

"Plant-based sausage. Sounds good." Anything Life chose sounded well above good, even anything plant-based disguised as meat.

"And it comes with cashew ricotta." She smacked her lips.

I rested my chin bone on my hand bone, gazing at her and sighing.

"What about you? Aren't you going to order?"

I snapped out of the sheer pleasure of looking at her flawless visage. "Me? Oh, yeah." I jiggled the menu in my hand bones. "Uh, I'll have the half dozen fresh oysters." Speaking in a wistful tone, I added, "I hear they're a natural aphrodisiac."

Life nodded politely and looked in the other direction.

The waiter arrived promptly and took our orders. Minutes later, he brought our sizzling hot food, which appeared as neatly arranged, bite-size morsels on massive white ceramic plates. Certainly, the tidbits were presented with impeccable style, but how did anyone feel satisfied eating at a five-star restaurant? I disregarded the minor irritation. All that mattered was Life and I had the hour to ourselves.

The tabletop candles flickered in their clear glass holders. The wax dripped bit by bit, seeming to slow down time. Golden lighting shone down upon our table, creating a soft, amorous mood—just what I'd hoped for. The La Next World restaurant was one of the most romantic in town. I'd personally selected it for that reason. Life didn't seem to mind—meaning she, too, secretly longed for me.

My skeleton grew slightly feverish.

Amid the hum of other entities chatting quietly around us, we started our small but extravagant meal. Ten minutes later, we'd cleaned our plates of the pappardelle Bolognese and oysters and now sipped our after-dinner drinks, me with a hard-hitting tequila and she with a smooth sherry.

The hard liquor relaxed my bones. With soft music playing, and having just downed a half-dozen oysters, now was the perfect time to bring my feelings out into the open, to savor the reciprocal love I'd secretly desired for centuries.

Preparing for the moment, I set my gaze on the candlelight, centered myself, and summoned the courage from the bottom of my abdominal cavity to tell Life how I feel. Then I took a long, deep breath.

"What a lovely restaurant," Life chirped, interrupting my plans. "I didn't know it was in the vicinity."

"Uh, yeah," I said, my speech slightly stilted. I felt a tension erupt in my expression. "It's new on the block. Just opened not too long ago." I shifted in my seat. Drats, a missed opportunity.

Life glanced around at the extravagant décor, including the Romantic paintings of passionate lovers entwined in one other that hung in embellished gold-tone frames. Her gaze settled on the wall sconces. No doubt she admired the mellow ambiance they effortlessly delivered.

As long as she sat in front of me, I still had a chance. A tightness formed around my eye sockets. I reached across the table to grasp her hand, but my flighty hand bones knocked her glass on its side, spilling the remaining sherry over the tablecloth.

"Ah!" Life jumped back.

"Sorry. Sorry," I said, grabbing a cloth napkin and dabbing the liquor.

I swallowed excessively as my rib cage tightened. Feeling a slight disconnect from what had just happened to what I aimed to do, I attempted to regain my composure.

Life, in her infectious state of calm, made it easy.

A minute later, I inhaled deeply. "Um, Life?"

She returned her attention from the wall paintings to me.

"Yes, Reaper?" Her finely trimmed eyebrows arched like perfect rainbows.

"I've got something important to tell you."

"You do? I'm the same way. I've got something I want to share with you."

My eye sockets popped. "You do?"

"Yes. After all the time we'd spent together, I've grown to really trust you. I feel I can tell you almost anything." Her smile filled me more than the pricey, miniscule dinner I'd just devoured.

I gulped. "Mm-hmm?"

This was the moment, *my* moment. She'd express her undying love for me. If I had a pulse, it would race. I was *it,* her true and lasting love. No longer would I be the lonesome reaper, pining hopelessly for Life forever, yearning for her warm embrace. Once she revealed how much she loved me, I'd feel whole, like buckwheat or bulgur, and joyful as a titmouse. I'd sing from the rooftops and feel my spirit soar.

It was time to make my move. I gingerly leaned toward her from across the table. One kiss to seal the deal for eternity.

My skull inched closer, ever so slow and steady, like a languishing snail on a mission to clinch the love of my existence. Just as I was about to plant one, she blurted out, "Death!"

"Huh?" I whipped my skull around. "Where?"

The last thing I needed was for the boss to find me with his woman.

"Death. I'd been wanting to speak to you about him."

"You have?"

She nodded enthusiastically. "I've been thinking, Reaper. He didn't need to schedule that tsunami. Maybe he was wrong. But he'd been right about a lot of other things before."

I slinked back in my chair, tilted my skull down, and frowned. "Like what?"

She bolted upright, as if struck with a jolt of energy. Her eyes brightened and her face grew animated. "Take the dinosaurs, for instance. I had a fallout with him about that too, before your time." She dropped her head into her hands. "I never wanted him to wipe them out. I'd taken so much time perfecting their immense size, their ferocity, and their longevity. But he decided to do away with them."

I stared at her flatly. Where was this going?

"He flung an asteroid, and my masterpieces, which endured for millions of years, were wiped out instantly." Her pretty little lips frowned.

A second later, her entire body perked up again. "But Death was so right. By eliminating the dinosaurs, no matter how much I felt attached to them, he made room for a new species."

"The humans?" I asked in the lowest, drabbest vocal pitch I'd used all evening. I was certain my eye sockets looked tired, because I suddenly lacked mental and physical energy.

She beamed. "Yes, people."

My chest cavity sank into my empty abdominal area.

For the rest of the evening, all Life talked about was Death. He did this and that, and shouldn't have done this but was right about that, and on and on ad infinitum.

My input apparently wasn't necessary during her nonstop discussions about Death's blunders and achievements. His glories received more air time than I cared to hear. She didn't seem to notice at all as I sat motionless, gazing down as she yapped on.

I laid my hand bone on my forehead bone and silently groaned.

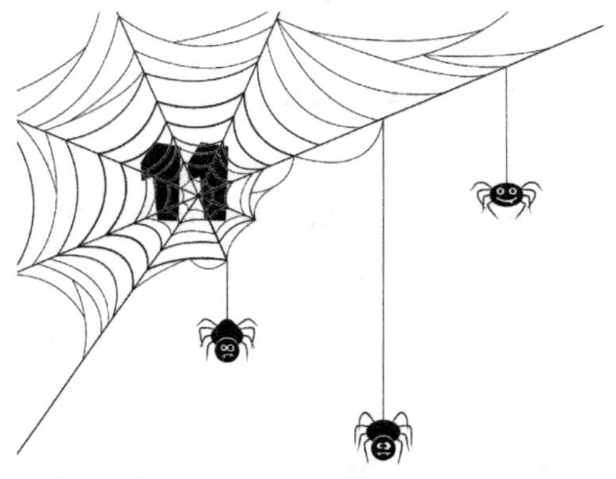

Life insisted we dine at the Earthbound DinDin Bistro for a change of scenery. It'd been one of Life's and Death's favorite Earthly haunts when they were on good terms. She'd said they'd been stimulated by its fantastical playground of senses: unique tastes, beautiful sights, soothing sounds, and luxurious feels.

Indeed, as I walked in, it felt nowhere as ethereal as the bistros in the next world, where time didn't exist and a welcome sense of peacefulness was the main entrée—except when you're clamoring after a love interest who shows no signs of reciprocation.

Proceeding farther into the dimly lit restaurant, we were enveloped by the tantalizing scent of fried tempura. Low dining tables filled the intimate space. Deep red cushions lay over the tatami, which I learned from Life were reed-like mats. My shoulder bones slumped slightly when I found out we were obligated to kneel in a *seiza* position on the mats—with our heels tucked under us.

I drew my breath in and released it before attempting the kneeling position. At once my leg bones released a *crack crack* sound. As a reaper who'd been more accustomed to steak frites and a frothy beer at a torn-up leather booth in the local mom and pop joint, this seating arrangement made my finger bones jitter. In no uncertain terms, it was a pain in the sit bones.

Life looked over at me with a flabbergasted smile. "You okay, Reaper?"

"Just fine. Carry on," I muttered, struggling to contort my leg bones into a position they hadn't been in for hundreds of years. I grimaced and swallowed. Gritting my teeth, I slanted my skeleton away from Life, hoping she wouldn't notice me fumbling and my ear bones turning red.

Nimble Life eased onto the cushions. Her knees sank effortlessly into the soft pillows, as if she'd done this a gazillion times. She smiled and rested her chin on her hand, watching me.

A few minutes and several attempts later, I managed to twist my leg bones into the required unnatural position. I let out a huge sigh and sat still as a wooden board. One false move and I might've found my bones creaking, causing Life undue concern again. Granted, at over seven hundred years, I was old, but I didn't want to *seem* old to the eternally youthful force before me.

A smiling waitress dressed in a black, floral kimono-style dress arrived, gave us a polite greeting, and dropped a pile of steamed white towels on our table. The steam wafted up from the hot cloths and hit me in the face bones. Instantly, I was transported to my own personal sauna. I basked in the sensation.

But, since turning red in the face bones after my ridiculous attempt to practice good seating etiquette, I decided they could use a good wipe-down. Maybe to remove all traces of my initial awkwardness.

As I brought the hot towel to my cheekbone, Life raised her palm and shouted, "No, Reaper!" She clasped her hand over her mouth.

I dropped the towel. "Wh-what?"

She pointed to the towel. "They're for wiping your hands, not your face. Never wipe your face with the towel," she said, shaking her head.

My skeleton sunk into itself. "Uh, okay."

Wasn't that what a hot towel was for? Maybe they did things differently in the material realm. Self-consciously, I cleaned my hand bones with the towel in preparation for the meal, which promised to be appetizing.

Sake was on the menu. I itched to get my hand bones on the delicious rice wine. I'd drink it straight and feel a little tipsy to make the evening go smoothly.

"I'll have the Ginjo-shu too," I said to the waitress, after Life had requested the same.

Then Life decided on a vegetable plate of silken tofu, mushrooms, and yuba. I placed an order for pork meatballs with a drizzle of olive oil, which sounded nothing short of delish. We handed our menus back to the cheerful waitress.

Our hot food arrived within minutes. We grabbed our chopsticks from the paper cup holder on the center of the table and dove in. At least Life devoured her meal with her chopsticks, while I struggled to skillfully maneuver the wooden sticks between my clunky finger bones to get one measly bite.

"The tofu is delicious," Life said with a mouthful, drizzling soy sauce over her plate.

I pointed my chopsticks at her. "These meatballs are seasoned perfectly." In reality, I referred to the delectable aroma of spices. I'd only had one nibble, considering my failed efforts to keep the pork in between the chopsticks long enough to deliver the morsel to my open jawbone.

Life eyed my nearly full plate. "You're not eating much today."

"He-he. I'm just taking my time," I replied with a smile, secretly wishing for a fork, or at least the ability to manipulate the chopsticks more fluidly.

Life finished off every last bit on her plate, then began admiring the abstract red and black geometric fish paintings that covered the nearby walls. In the meantime, my plate remained mostly uneaten. I had a mind to dig into the meatballs with my finger bones and avoid the hassle of using chopsticks, but I wanted to impress Life with my fine dining etiquette.

Out of the blue, shrill laughter shattered the quiet, peaceful ambiance of the restaurant. Life glanced over at the loud crowd that had just walked in. Her eyes grew big as the saucers in front of me. Her lips began to curl, as if she wanted to say something but couldn't find the words.

"Look at that. He's got nerve!" she said at last, pulling her body back in disgust. She crossed her arms, turned her chin up and the other way, and snorted. It was a beautiful snort, though.

I twisted my neck bones to see what in the afterworld she was referring to. I'm sure I went even whiter in the face bones because there was Death amidst this flashy, boisterous group, striding with swagger in the company of several overly bejeweled Earthly females.

One of the women, alive as can be, threw her arm around Death's muscular shoulders and hung onto him for dear life. Her lips were painted cherry red, and her eyes were lined heavily in onyx. Her overpowering perfume made me wish I could shut my naval cavity, even from four tables and a five-foot bamboo divider away.

I wanted to turn to Life to ask her if she saw what I saw. But she was busy pouting and still looking the other way, as if to suppress a torrent of tears. I blinked rapidly at the frolicky females and Death.

Death smile and laughed, clearly enjoying the company and attention of these heavily painted women.

Oddly, I recognized the perfumed woman. I'd seen her before when I picked up scheduled souls on various television sets. She was an A-list actress who'd made waves on the silver screen. She'd starred in several movies, a handful of television shows, and a few national commercials. She'd made a name for herself as a sultry femme fatale who'd take 'em, shake 'em, and break 'em.

I looked down, snapping my finger bones, trying to recall her name.

In his booming voice, Death said, "Leona Anci, you're a star. Everyone adores you. Even me!"

Leona stroked Death's smiling lips with her index finger. "Oh, you're too much, darling."

Life grabbed the fabric of her dress in a fist. Her mouth dropped open, but no words escaped. Instead, she let out a disdainful scoff. Then she turned her face away, raising her hands to cover it. Clearly, she didn't want to see the drama unfolding in front of her.

What the devil was going on in this little bistro, tucked away in the middle of the Earthly sphere? Death took pleasure in the embrace of another woman—an earthly female, at that, who didn't hold a candle to the breathtaking force sitting across from me. How could he betray Life? Something didn't add up.

I watched the group as they kneeled chaotically on the cushions they'd scattered, all the while chortling and chitchatting nonstop about nothing of importance. Within moments, they'd ordered several bottles of Japanese lager. Each of them had a bottle for themselves and drank heartily.

Gregarious and bubbly, the group failed to notice Life and me in our quiet corner.

"Let's leave," Life grumbled, already standing up and grabbing her purse.

"Um, okay."

I somehow hoisted my skeleton up without breaking anything. As we rushed out, I glanced back at Death being amused by the chattering women. I needed to get to the bottom of this bizarreness.

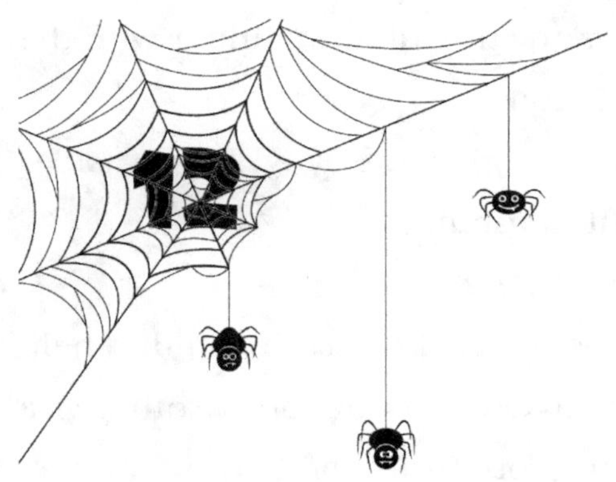

12

"Of course, darling," Leona Anci said breathily to someone on the other end of her phone. "I've got him wrapped around my finger. Everything's going as planned."

Hovering over Leona's living room couch like an apparition, my brow bone arched. Who did she have wrapped around her finger? And what plans? I shivered in my bones. Something in the air smelled putrid.

One perk of belonging to the next world was having the ability to straddle the earthly sphere at any point in time. I could travel from the worldly realm to the next without a hitch. It was like maneuvering from the kitchen to the dining room while balancing a silver salver on the tips of my fingerbones. Easy-peasy. And this is exactly what I did today to dig into the mysterious persona of this Leona Anci, to find out what she was up to in regard to Death and, by extension, my lovely Life.

"He'll do anything for an autograph or dinner with the A-listers." She cackled hideously.

At the sound of her nasally laughter, my empty insides turned, making me want to vomit.

What buffoon would be so naïve?

I leaned in to hear better. As I did so, I couldn't help but to notice the ten golden Oscar statues on the otherwise empty shelves, the numerous full-length oval mirrors she clearly needed to serve as personal reminders of her absolute greatness, and the vase of dead flowers atop a stack of books she'd probably never read.

She twirled her long, dry bleached blond hair that had been curled at the tips. "I'm sure of it. I've already bought myself countless more weeks. All I had to do was take him out to dinner with the girls. He lapped up our company like a thirsty puppy."

My empty eye sockets nearly burst out of my skull. I swiveled my neck bone and brought my finger bone to my parted jaw.

Dinner with the girls? She bought herself more time?

There was only one phantasm who had the power to give anyone more time. Only one otherworldly force that could extend her stay in the earthly sphere—or shorten it. I shook my jawbone to clear my skull. But the reality stuck: Death was being used like a dirty rag.

How could one of the two most powerful forces in the universe fall for this shameless scam? Granted, Death had become weakened by his constant fighting with Life. The stress of all the arguments had compelled him toward the bottle, and he hadn't yet gotten a breather. Certainly, he wasn't thinking right either.

Just as Life was unbearably lonely, Death was too. Despite being polar opposites, they were one and the same. Life and Death needed each other, like yin needs yang or bait needs a hook or a hamburger needs a toasted sesame bun. He craved attention—and if this masculine powerhouse didn't get it from Life, he'd resort to getting it from elsewhere. Being a fellow myself, I understood.

I snapped my finger bones. *Drats!* Death was in deep trouble.

He'd become dangerously gullible in his enfeebled state, falling for ploys like this from the incorrigible, pompous Leona Anci and her equally disdainful gal crew. He was like a crying baby who could be soothed with a lollipop from the dime store.

So long as Death enjoyed nights out with this distasteful earthly female, Life would remain blue. Her sullenness hit me in the rib cage like a bullet at close range.

Worsening matters, the earthly realm couldn't survive for long under such dire conditions, thereby affecting my role as reaper of the dead. Death being manipulated to extend life didn't bode well for Earth. And Life being too blue to create more life didn't either. With a lack of death and a lack of life, the whole scheme of earthly existence would inevitably topple on itself.

"I could live forever," Leona said. "Just a stroke of his cheek and a whisper in his ear and he'd stop at nothing to make my wishes come true." She didn't seem to mind stooping low to take advantage of the boss and further her prospects at life.

I snooped around her house as she yakked on. Fresh roses filled every room. I glanced at the attached cards, which were scribbled with men's names: Tommy, Ned, Allen, Dirk, and on and on. Unopened, heart-shaped boxes of chocolates lay scattered on the countertops. Stuffed animals holding fuzzy red hearts lined the shelves in her bedroom. Gifts from her many admirers.

A sickened feeling overwhelmed my bones. Leona Anci was a highly sought-after actress. She'd never be so admired in the afterworld—it was too competitive, with the likes of the violet-eyed Elizbeth Taylor and the fiercely intelligent Queen Cleopatra demanding every hungry male's attention. No wonder Leona wanted stay in the earthly sphere. Lengthening her lifespan, even through sheer manipulation, was the only way she'd get to continue living the high life.

By bribing Death in his vulnerable state, Leona had made sure she never made it on my list.

The debauchery made my insides flip flop. Even I had scruples.

The problematic, soul-sucking client returns continued nonstop.

I delivered a winsome soul to its next phase of existence when Moe stumbled out of the typical nowhere. His hairy, animalistic hands clutched a soul of breathtaking beauty. Her oval face appeared serene, as if she'd just returned from an all-day luxury spa. Her skin looked rejuvenated, with not one sign of stress on her visage. Her slender limbs hung relaxed at her sides. Her auburn hair shone like it'd been pampered with a revitalizing egg-white wash. The soul must've been thirty-five but appeared a lithe twenty-five. She glowed like an ethereal being, fittingly.

"Same deal, Moe?" I asked, pulling my boat up close to the banks.

"You got it, Reaper," the spirit guide replied in his usual gruff manner. "She needs to go back pronto." Shaking his head, which jiggled his beard, he grumbled, "I don't know when this nonsense will stop."

Per his characteristic rudeness, he pushed the gentle soul forward, then flapped his big hand in dismissal. Judging by his rough treatment of returned souls, he obviously didn't believe the return process was worth the monumental effort of escorting them back then patiently waiting for my arrival.

"Uh, I don't know either. Hopefully soon." I caught her in the nick of time by the arm before she landed in the frigid river, then eased her onto my boat. In the wake of all his distractions, Death never got around to pointing out the spirit guide's blatant failures in customer service.

Moe turned, palms thrown up loosely, as if to say, "Who cares?", then disappeared into the fog as he always did.

"So, how was it?" I asked the soul, attempting to make chitchat. A little banter made the boat ride more congenial. Otherwise, it'd have been a cold, uncomfortably silent, and dreary trip back to the other side.

She wrapped her arms around herself, hugging her knees to her chest, and let out a happy squeal. An animated smile crossed her face and stayed there as she spoke. "I'd never imagined, but being there changed my life. I've undergone a one-eighty-degree transformation."

My brow bone arched. "Oh? Not a three-sixty?"

"Then I'd be right where I started," she said, laughing at my sorry attempt at humor.

"Well, you'll literally be right where you started in a few minutes time." I eyed the destination. At my pace of three miles per hour, with no wind to disturb the surface of the river, it'd take exactly that long.

"You know what I mean," she jested.

The soul's amber eyes sparkled as she let go of herself and leaned forward off the wooden seat. Her palms lay flat on the bottom of the boat. She tried standing up.

"No, no. No standing on the boat," I warned. "I'm not responsible for hoisting souls who've fallen off the boat. I've got no training in it, and the boat's never been equipped with life jackets."

"All right." She slumped back in her seat. A second later, she grew animated again, quirking her eyebrows and smiling. Her pleasantness was rather refreshing. Normally, once a soul tasted the bliss of the afterlife, they resisted going back to the dismal status quo of earthly life. But she was a different beast.

"Reaper, you know what? I've been healed." Her head tipped back as she closed her eyes and brought her palms to her chest. "Completely healed."

"How so?"

"You picked me up in a horrible condition." Her voice grew quiet and monotone. "I'd overdosed on heroin. My lips and fingernails had turned blue. My body temperature had grown frigid." Her chin trembled as she described the awful scene to which I'd been summoned.

"I remember," I said, continuing to row through the cold water. The boat creaked steadily, adding a further eeriness to our candid conversation.

"Then..." Her mouth grew wide, and she gestured with her hands, as if introducing me to a whole new magical world. "I arrived at the other side."

She threw her arms up in a victory V, which rocked the boat slightly.

"Mm-hmm." I plunged my oar deeper into the water, bending my knee bones to balance the boat.

Oblivious to the unsteadiness her excitement caused, she continued her story.

"My battered, painful body was led to a healing pool. At first, I scoffed at the concept. Nothing could heal a desperate case like mine. I thought I had nothing to lose. So, I cautiously dipped my toe in. Reaper, do you know it was so warm? Like a grandmother's hug!"

"No, I never knew." I'd never had a grandmother, to my knowledge. If I did, I was sure she wouldn't have been a hugger.

"I submerged myself in the pool. At once, a feeling of rejuvenation overcame me. I was like a brand-new person. The steam floated up, and all the rapid bubbles eased my aching body. I stayed in the healing pool for hours, never wanting to leave that delightful place, before they told me it was time to go back." She tugged at the bottom edge of my cloak like a child wanting to tell her mother what a fantastic day she had. "But I'm no longer an addict. I've been miraculously healed. I can feel it!"

"Nice. You're going back a healed person. Couldn't ask for more than that."

"It's been the highlight of my afterlife!" She started to cry happy tears and laugh at the same time. I'd have been inclined to think she was bonkers if it hadn't been for her telling me her touching story.

At the banks of the earthly realm, the cheery soul sprang off the boat with both feet. Embracing her newly healthy body and mind, she hopped and skipped away without a care in the world and snapped back into her body, sprawled out on the floor. I shook my skull and sighed with satisfaction. It was always a bonus for everybody in earthly existence when the next world did incredible favors like that.

I gave my list a brief glance. My next client didn't need to be picked up in the Mediterranean for a couple of hours. It gave me enough time to contemplate what I'd do about Life.

With breathlessness, I sped back to headquarters.

Life sat there in her office, with her mess of soft, red curls falling over her desk. She looked entranced. Her half-shuttered eyelids didn't blink. I kept hearing her sigh through her luscious fuchsia lips. She stared at the computer screen, but she didn't type anything.

The sight tugged at my empty rib cage. I was unwilling to leave her like that, but what could I do?

Grabbing a cup of coffee from the nearby break room, I swigged it down in one gulp. It did little to ease my angst, so I ventured back for more. I held the entire steaming pot in my hand bones, hoping that drinking copious amounts of the brew would lessen my worries.

Life couldn't work in her pathetic, saddened emotional state. If she did, potential blunders in creation could occur, from defects to missing body parts. I'd seen one too many birds born without wings lately, or a couple extra toes on the paws of dogs. Granted, Life adored every creation she produced equally, but none needed to suffer. Creation was at stake if she remained glum and distracted.

I scratched my skull. A difficult decision lay before me.

Clearly, Life remained amorously in love with Death. I couldn't get one kiss out of her even under the most idyllic romantic conditions. All she ever talked about was him. There was no way in eternity she'd give him up for me, no matter how badly she mourned their relationship. And Death was painfully lonely without Life, evidenced by his drinking, partying with the wrong crowd, and dire mistakes in scheduling.

I could never replace the romantic escapades I'd enjoyed with Life: our intimate candle-lit dinners, exhilarating bike rides through the winding countryside, and catching comedic theatrical plays now and then. Though I grew weak in the knee bones on every date, spending alone time with her meant the afterworld to me. She gave me the gift of companionship. I was aware of nothing else when she was near. But truth be told: I didn't have a shot. Life cared too deeply about Death. His feelings were mutual.

Being a rickety third wheel was the best a lanky reaper could do. Even as we passed through the infinite bounds of eternity, I'd still be that "extra guy" no one genuinely wanted.

I stood tall, thrusting my rib cage out and taking a long, ponderous breath. A higher priority was in order. I needed to make the afterworld—and by extension the world—right again.

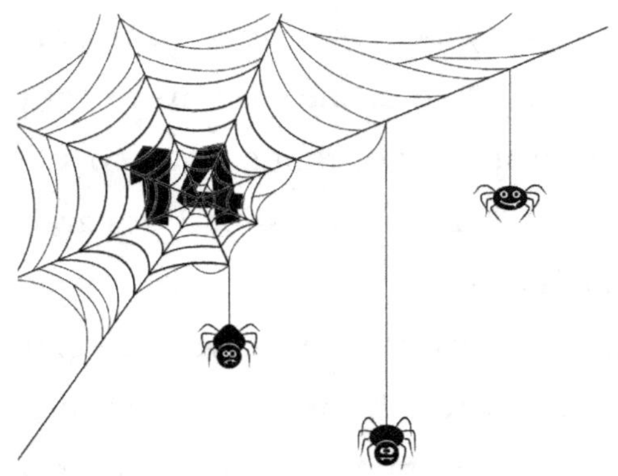

Two hours passed in the blink of an eye socket. I rushed to the picturesque beaches of the Mediterranean, where I'd be picking up my next client in a palatial Portofino mansion, three stories high with a view of the sea from its numerous bay windows.

As soon as I stepped my foot bone on the shore, my skeleton froze. I broke out in a cold sweat without knowing why. It was like an instinctual response to something dreadful.

This place looked familiar, uncannily familiar. It took me a while to jog my memory. Then it hit me. How could I have forgotten? Barely by the skin of my teeth, I'd escaped from the long pier next to this very mansion. I recalled the sordid morning clearly, me in my black cloak and she in her crop top wedding gown. I'd leapt into the sea to avoid a dreaded marriage.

I began to heave, feeling rooted to the sand beneath my feet bones. If I had veins, I was sure they'd pulse visibly. My elbow bones pressed against my side, I made myself as small as possible.

In the midst of my overwhelming terror, I had to make sure I wasn't imagining things. My arm bones shaking, I brought out my list and checked it. There, in bold letters, was my next client's name: Elvira.

Examining the schedule, I became aware of her cause of death. She'd drowned in a bathtub full of bubbles. Apparently, she'd lost her rubber ducky somewhere in the suds, leaned down to retrieve it, and breathed in the bubbles. She'd choked for several minutes before succumbing, without ever retrieving her yellow ducky.

Lucky ducky. It narrowly escaped her clutches too!

Expelling an audible breath, I laid my splayed hand bones over my rib cage and looked up to the blue sky. How could Death do this to me? I'd barely escaped Elvira's grasp once before. Now the boss had put me in a precarious position with this fanatic gothic vamp hell-bent on making me hers forever.

I coughed and heaved over again. This just couldn't *be*, I repeated to myself. I loosened my grip, and my smartphone dropped into the sand with a light thud. I'd grown too weak-boned to pick it up.

My toe bones curling and digging into the granules of sand, I pondered my horrible fate. If I endeavored to whisk Elvira's soul to the other side, I'd be trapped, alone with her on my boat for several agonizing minutes. How would I manage? With the river surrounding me in every direction, I had no escape route.

The boss confused me. The only logical explanation was that every soul on Earth had to eventually pass. But honestly, Elvira, and now? Amid all these soul returns? When I was already flustered?

I shrugged weakly. My ribs felt too tight. I felt hollowed out, though I literally was.

But as a reaper, I had a job to do, whether it involved Elvira or some other foul creature from the fathomless depths of the dark lagoon.

Though time slowed to a halt, I decided it was a momentary nuisance to transport Elvira's soul. It'd be over and done, at best, within a matter of minutes, or send me into the bottomless pit of disgust at worst. Clenching my teeth, I shuffled ever so slowly up the beach and toward her mansion.

Slightly put off by the winged dragon door knocker, I mustered the courage to make my presence known. I cautiously wrapped my cold finger bones around the fearsome knocker and knocked thrice on the massive front door.

"Um, hello? Anyone home?"

No answer.

I inched the door open with a bellowing creak. I shuddered and crept up the stairs to the second floor. The bathroom door stood ajar, enough to peek my skull inside.

"Ciao, Elvira?"

Still no answer, likely because she was dead.

A bubble floated up toward my face bones. I flicked it, causing it to pop and spray soap in every direction. I cursed under my breath.

Then my ear bones picked up a shrill voice. I cringed.

"*Amore, mio*. You've come!"

Turning my skull slowly, I came face bone to face with Elvira's dastardly soul. She hovered above the bathtub, her pudgy arms outstretched and her lips puckered, as if awaiting a kiss.

My skeleton shrank back. But I grew emboldened by remembering I had duties to perform.

"Now listen, Elvira. This is purely business. No hanky panky while I transport your soul." Being upfront might set the course right. But I was dealing was Elvira, and reason didn't jive with her.

"But *amore*, I always knew you'd come back." She lunged toward me, like an angry sea witch surfacing from the ocean's darkest depths, attempting to wrap her arms around my quivering skeleton.

I ducked swiftly, missing her deathly cold embrace. I let out a quick breath of relief.

Taking a cue from Moe, I grabbed her by the arm, intending to lead her toward my boat. Instead of resisting, she came willingly, almost as if she took pleasure in my cold hand bones grasping her.

"My love, I feel how you desire me." She batted her onyx lashes. "We shall spend eternity together, you and me. It'll be *amore* forever."

I swallowed hard and violently rolled my shoulder bones. She stepped onto the boat, which plunged it so deep into the river that water flooded the seating area.

I grunted. More cleanup for me to do amid my already packed schedule. The boat had to remain well-maintained for the sake of good customer service, which was so highly prized in the afterworld.

Elvira made herself comfortable in the seat at the opposite end. I pushed the boat away from the banks with my tip of my oar and began to row.

"This is like taking a ride on a gondola in Venice, no?" She smiled her black-lipstick smile and pointed at me with her midnight-black fingernail—a worrisome come-hither gesture that would've made me throw up, had it not been for the fact that my insides were empty.

The murky, dark water didn't seem like a Venetian canal in the least. And I certainly didn't feel like a romantic gondolier. I didn't have the striped shirt with the leisurely tied red scarf, the snazzy matching hat, the quirky dark mustache, or the latent singing talent.

"Sing for me, *amore mio*," she demanded anyway.

"What?" I pointed to my rib cage. "Who, me?"

"Yes, you, *amore*. You will delight me by singing a song of love, *our* eternal love."

I grew quiet and fidgeted with my hand bones. She stomped her foot against the bottom of the boat, cracking the wood. Then, with steam shooting out of her ears, she commanded with a scream, "Now!"

I glanced to my left and to my right. With the river surrounding me in all directions, escape wasn't possible. Slowly, I dropped my jaw and began to muster a low tune. My voice came out crackly.

"Uh, a-amore, nothin' but amore," I started, somewhat crooning.

Elvira leaned back and closed her dark eyes.

"You're out of tune," she snapped, popping her eyes open.

"I am? Well, singing is not my thing. It's not even part of the passage. See—"

"Singing will be part of *my* passage!" she thundered. "Understand, *amore mio*?" A soft smile replaced whatever was left of her volcanic eruption from a second before.

I shuddered, hoping the banks of the next world would be in sight soon.

Minutes of my warbly singing passed. My song came out more like a strangled cry of frustration, but she didn't notice.

Finally, the edges of eternity appeared. I wiped my brow bone and exhaled, believing I'd jumped the biggest hurdle of my seven-hundred-year career.

"Okay, Elvira. Your stop. See ya," I said, thinking I'd wiped my hand bones clean of her.

She stared at me with wide eyes and scoffed. "My stop? No, *amore*," she cried out, shaking her head. "*Our* stop!"

Elvira grabbed me by the cloak and dragged me off the boat and into the shallow water. I kicked and fought back with all my strength.

"What're you doing?"

"We're going to eternity together!"

"It's not my place. I've got a job to do," I screamed back, still resisting her.

With arms as powerful as a quarterback's, she yanked my feeble skeleton like a child pulling a little red wagon down the street.

"Stop! Help!" I shouted to anyone who'd listen.

Moe came running out of the woodwork. I'd never been so happy to see him. He stopped momentarily and watched our struggle. From the corner of my eye sockets, as Elvira had me in a chokehold, I swore I saw him laugh.

I turned to the spirit guide. "Moe, help me!"

His big arms overpowering her, he dragged her away, still kicking and screaming, "But *amore mio*! What about our passionate love?"

Exhaling, I collected myself and straightened out my tattered cloak. What a close brush with doom. As I picked up my oar, it dawned on me that Elvira might be among the continual soul returns. I'd have to deal with her twice more if Death made another gargantuan mistake.

The possibility hit me hard. I began taking rapid shallow breaths, gulping the air like none was left.

Vowing not to be in this appalling position a second time, I made it my mission to intervene in Death's abominable drinking—stat.

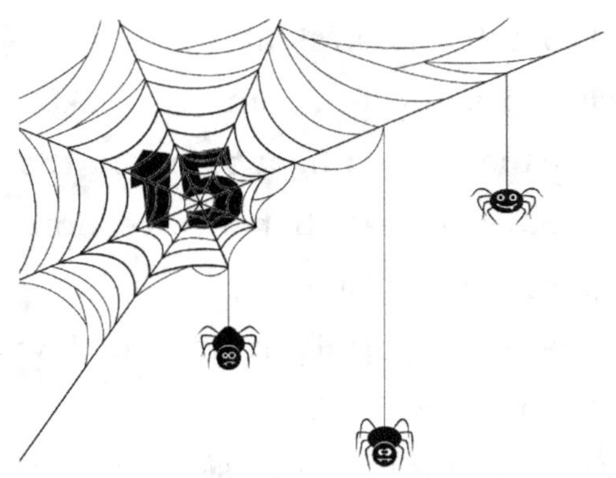

I rapped on Death's office door with a tightness in my rib cage. My well-thought-out plan may or may not work. I'd settled the final details last night, careful not to miss any possibility of it turning into an outright fiasco. If it failed, I was doomed to a hellscape of infinite soul returns—and, even worse, being in the suffocating goth-clutches of Elvira. Plus, Life would remain in tears, leaving me absorbing her poignant sadness and feeling blue myself.

Mind whirring with all the possible ways Death would shoot down my plans, I cleared my throat and asked, "Boss?"

His booming voice ricocheted off the four office walls. "What is it, Reaper?"

Pushing the door open farther, I poked my skull in. Fortunately, my nasal cavity wasn't hit by overpowering whiffs of intoxicating liquor, signaling to me that, for now, the boss was sober.

Now was the perfect time to intervene.

I pushed the door open and stood partially inside. "Do you have a minute?"

"Make it quick, Reaper. What is it?" He didn't even look up at me, instead fiddling with papers on his desk.

My gaze didn't settle on the boss either. In fact, I avoided direct eye contact. "See, I've noticed that everyone in the office is a little stressed lately."

"Mm-hmm." He turned swiftly to glare at me, as if I'd upset him. Did I? The last thing I wanted was to upset one of the most powerful forces in the known universe, a force who could crush me in an instant and scatter my dust particles like a heating and air conditioning system. My bones quivered.

"Um, I've noticed a sort of weary vibe in the office. Things aren't like they should be." My sweaty hand bones began fidgeting with the round brass doorknob. I felt it loosening, almost to the point of falling off. I quickly jerked my hand bone away and wiped my sweat on my cloak.

"And?" came his apathetic reply.

"It gave me the bright idea of a staff vacation. We'd all be refreshed taking a few days off. Soak up the sunshine and get a bit of vitamin D. Maybe lounge by the refreshing sea. He-he."

Ending with a laugh gave me the excuse to say I was joking—in case he felt a sudden urge to rip my skull off.

"You do, huh?"

I looked at the boss in a daze. Death wasn't totally put off by my suggestion. It was the golden hour of opportunity, and I wasn't about to miss it. Almost bouncing on my toe bones, I whipped out two brochures from my cloak pocket.

"See, here? It's the Soul Freedom Islands. It'd do us good to spend four days without disruption from anyone. Picture it." I spread my hand bones wide in front of me. "No complaints from unhappy souls or even cantankerous spirit guides. Peace, nature, and tranquility await us. What have we got to lose?"

I flashed him a thousand-watt smile to sweeten the deal.

Death grunted. His thick eyebrow arched.

I almost felt my meticulously laid-out plans falling through the empty spaces between my hand bones into the dark void. It was essential to up the ante with a bit of enthusiasm.

"The spark of the afterlife will return. Daily operations will improve. It'd be a great morale booster for the whole team." I eyed him, hoping my logic and zealous presentation would be convincing.

He leaned back in his swivel chair and crossed his arms over his massive chest.

"You've got a point there, Reaper."

"I do?" I jerked my skull back. "I mean, of course I do." I slapped the glossy travel brochures and tickets down on his desk.

"The vacay starts tomorrow."

"What?"

"Yeah, I've already made the plans. All you, I mean we, need to do is show up. It's an all-expense paid trip, courtesy of my generous employee expense report. Hope you don't mind the exorbitant charge."

Cowering, I gave him a cheesy smile.

Death inhaled long and deep. A small smile crept across his face. "Reaper, this is why I like having you on my team."

"So, you'll go?"

Appearing relaxed, he smiled bigger and sat up straight. "I'll be there. Hope to see you there too."

"Uh, I'll be there, all right." I inched away from his doorway. "Thanks, boss. This means a lot."

Feeling light as air, I rushed to my next stop: Life's office.

She answered when I knocked. "Yes, Reaper?"

I proposed the same deal to Life, whose eyes brightened like twinkling stars.

"Great. See you tomorrow. By the way, you look lovely in green."

She responded with a coy smile and returned her attention to her paperwork.

A luxurious weightlessness overcame my bones. I wanted to let out a happy holler, but opted for professionalism instead. This so-called staff vacay couldn't have been easier to put into action.

I stepped off the boat, greeted by the lush green flora and fauna of the Soul Freedom Islands. The beach seemed to stretch for endless miles. Palm trees danced in the temperate breeze. The water appeared clear and blue as sapphires under fluorescent lighting.

I eyed the small seaside home in the distance where the vacay would take place.

“Greetings!” said a quiet, feathery voice.

I turned to see a thin spectacled being, probably five feet tall when I accounted for his hunch. Transparent as sunshine, he wore a wrinkly smile that gave him an eccentric grandfatherly look.

“Uh, hello. You must be Mr. Bottman.”

“Indeed, I am. And you good sir?”

“Reaper. They call me Reaper.” I stretched out my hand bone, and he shook it. “So, have the guests arrived?”

Mr. Bottman looked toward the shore as two luxury super yachts sped through the water toward the island. “I think our guests are arriving as we speak.”

“Great. I’ll duck out. You know what to do.”

“I certainly do. I’ve been researching relationships for centuries. They don’t call Soul Freedom Islands the perfect spot for a couple’s retreat for no reason. Au revoir, Reaper!”

He waved as I took my position behind the swaying palm trees.

Death stepped off his yacht and stretched his arms wide. Then Life exited her yacht and exhaled.

Upon seeing Life, the boss momentarily froze. She, in turn, pressed her fist to her mouth. From my hidden perch, their shocked expressions were as clear as day.

Mr. Bottman approached Death and Life and shook their hands.

"Couple's retreat?" Death bellowed. His deafening roar caused several palm tree fronds to loosen and fall on my crouching skeleton, poking me hard. Grimacing, I shook them off.

Life crossed her arms, turned up her chin, and looked the other way, huffing.

"I didn't sign up for a couple's retreat!" Death snarled, flexing his large arm muscles. "Wait 'til I get my hands on Reaper."

I shivered in my hideout post.

Mr. Bottman smiled. "Well since you're already here, and the yachts are on their way back, why don't you come inside?" He gestured for them to follow.

Death's nostrils flared. Cracking his knuckles, he and Life stomped down the sandy path toward the seaside house, where their couple's counseling was scheduled to begin.

Life and Death took their seats on opposite sides of the orange 1570s style sofa.

"Over the next four days, you'll both learn the foundations of a healthy relationship," Mr. Bottman said, with the patience of someone who'd dealt with difficult personalities for eons. "We'll role play real afterlife scenarios, so you can practice the skills you'll learn and strengthen your relationship." He paused to look at their stunned faces. "How does that sound?"

Death grumbled and rolled his eyes.

During the cleverly disguised retreat, Life and Death steadily gained the skills they needed to bolster their friendship, spice up their everlasting romance, and deepen their understanding of each other.

Swinging lazily in the hammock outside, I heard Death's voice thunder, "What d'you mean I kill off too many life forms?"

Almost instinctually, as in an act of self-preservation, my leg bones perked up, prepared to run.

Unlike me, Mr. Bottman remained undeterred by Death's fury and intervened. He handed Life a tissue and instructed calmly, "Now, Life, you must express your feelings. Honesty is the best policy. Let's keep the conflict discussion constructive." He smiled like an affectionate grandpa.

Dabbing the corners of her eyes, Life sniffled. "Each of my creations means everything to me. You keep shortening their lifespans. I've spent so much effort on them. It's unfair!"

"It's my job, remember?"

"Yes, but you can give them more time."

Mr. Bottman interrupted again. "This is a great moment to unearth the values each of you has, and the afterlife purposes you both share." He stepped back, like a referee letting the match go on.

Death skidded across the sofa closer to Life and threw his arm around her shoulders. Tilting his head, he spoke softly. "If it means that much to you, I'll give them all the time you want."

Life glanced up, her eyes shining brighter than ever. "You will?"

"Yes, I will."

She hugged him, and he hugged her back tightly.

"Compromises are the key to breaking through conflict," Mr. Bottman said, giving them a round of applause. "Well done."

The rest of the retreat proceeded smoothly, with fewer and fewer angry outbursts from Death and less crying from Life. By the end of the four days, Death and Life became inseparable, wrapped in each other's embrace as they walked along the beach or toasted bubbly champagne on starry nights. It appeared their everlasting affection for each other had been restored.

As a simple reaper at the bottom of the workplace hierarchy, I may never have had the ability to light Life's fire like Death. But it made me tingly to see her invested and joyful again. It was what the world needed—a spirited force behind all of creation.

I wiped a small tear away, then dry wiped my hand bones.

Mission accomplished.

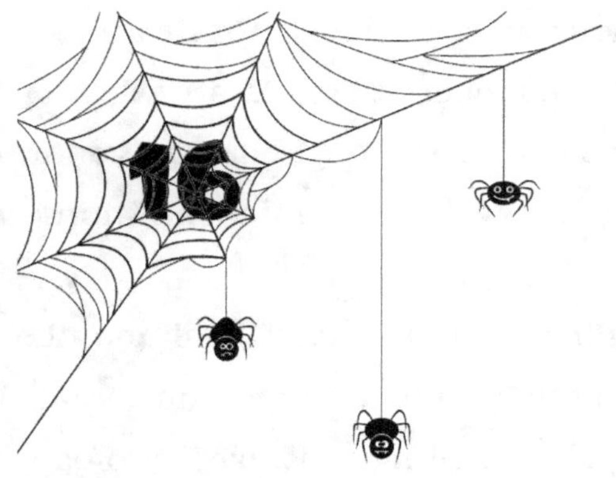

After returning from the couple's retreat, Life waltzed gracefully through the office like a prima ballerina assoluta. She held her chin up, her countenance radiating an enviable serenity. She no longer released deep, hopeless sighs or stared vacantly at her computer screen like she was lost in some dismal afterworld where joy was nonexistent. When she smiled, it reached her stunning green eyes.

She chitchatted with the rest of the employees, swapping recipes, asking about their weekends, and complimenting them on their unique fashion choices.

In other words, things were back to usual. On my rounds across the world, no longer did I see cockatiel parrots born with scissor beaks or newborn giraffes without spots. The grand scheme of worldly life had returned to its joyous heights. With my hand bone pressed against my rib cage, I uttered a silent thanks.

Never did I think the same could be said for Death.

Empty liquor bottles no longer littered Death's desk or office. Whenever I poked my skull through the boss's door, I wasn't hit in the face bones by the strong stench of mind-bending alcohol.

The messy scheduling of the past several months had taken its unwanted toll on me. But the familiar state of affairs had returned, and I clung to it like Styrofoam peanuts to a cardboard box.

In the middle of headquarters, I stood still as the dead, letting the relief sink in. The next moment, I felt the urge to jump up and down with the sheer exhilaration of the return of the status quo.

I was most excited about my schedule, now manageable once more. The soul returns had gradually died down. Granted, it wasn't an immediate correction, as things involving life and death were never instant and needed to slowly get back to where they were—which took time.

For the most part, Moe no longer greeted me at the shore on every other occasion I delivered a soul. It was just me and my clients, whom I left on the blissful banks of eternity. Without being burdened by unwilling souls who had to be returned to life, I was then on my merry way. In fact, I began to miss encountering the crotchety spirit guide, who'd been a major part of my job for a long, disastrous while.

The unbearable heat of the soul returns had cooled. I began noticing the roses, smelling their fragrant blooms again. My vodka glass stood half full these days.

The afterworld was right again.

One fine day, I checked my schedule. A familiar name caught my attention: Leona Anci.

I slapped my hand bones against my cheekbones. Her time had been long overdue, thanks to her deceitful practices, bribes, and flattery.

But Death, the capable boss I'd known for eons, was no longer desperate for affection and easily manipulated by any such seasoned seductress. He'd come to his good senses and put this A-list actress where she belonged—at the top of my list.

On a dusty western movie set, with rickety taverns to my left and flourishing cacti to my right, I swooped down. Leona sat in front of a mirror in the dressing room, the door of which featured her name in gold letters above a sparkly star. She powdered her face white as a ghost as I made my grand entrance. With curlers in her bleach-blond hair and wearing a pink silk robe, she never expected me.

"Leona Anci, you're coming with me," I said in a steady, low-pitched voice, and in no uncertain terms.

She glanced up, still holding the powder puff. "Excuse me? Do you know who I am?"

"Yes, ma'am. Ms. Anci, you're a famous movie star, but that doesn't stop me from collecting your soul, which you gave up anyway by chasing fame above all else."

She parted her red lips and scoffed. "Now you listen here, Reaper. I've got connections in high places. You best beware. Leona Anci calls the shots."

"I'm well aware of the connections you've paid handsomely for. How shall I put it? Extravagant dinners and drinks, the company of glamorous people, the shameless flattery. But your bribes and schemes aren't as effective now, are they?"

Leona slammed her powder puff into the container, sending white particles hurling into the air. I waved my hand bones in front of my skull, trying not to inhale the big clouds of powder.

In her rage, she flew up from the chair, painted claws out, ready to pounce. But before she laid a fingernail on me, she gasped, clutched the left side of her chest, and fell flat on the floor.

"Eh." I checked my digital watch. "Heart attack, right on time."

I collected her soul and whisked her away to the other side. She sat in the boat, holding a pocket-size mirror and adding the finishing touches to her red lips. I smiled to myself as I rowed steadily through the river. She'd never have an opportunity to brazenly take advantage of Death again.

Once we approached the shores of eternity, Moe appeared out of the fog.

I shuffled back a step or two in the boat. What was he doing here? Surely, it couldn't have been another soul return. Maybe once in a while a straggler had to be returned. But for the most part, those had died down to almost nil.

Moe ambled toward the edge of the banks. As I neared, it was clear he didn't have a soul on his arm. Instead, he carried what looked like a pen and a pad of paper.

I scratched at my temple.

The spirit guide motioned for me to row faster. Uncertain as to what needed urgent attention, I maneuvered the boat as swiftly as I could. After all, an emergency might've awaited me.

Moe strode through the water, knee-deep, which he'd never done for any soul before. Leaning in, he took Leona gently by the arms and helped her out.

"Darling, you're too much," she said in response to his gesture of chivalry.

"Leona, I'm your biggest fan. Do you mind?" He pushed his pad of paper and pen toward her. "An autograph, if you please?"

Please? The spirit guide had never uttered *please* or any other niceties in any of our prior dealings. He lacked all sense of courtesy, pushing ordinary souls around and letting them fall into the river. Now, clearly, he was smitten, and reduced to a spineless lovebug.

Leona grabbed the pen and paper and scribbled on it. She pushed her sunglasses up the bridge of her nose and, chin in the air, let herself be escorted by dear old Moe. With my jaw dropped, I watched as she disappeared into the hazy glow of the next realm.

I stuck my hand bones into my tattered cloak pockets and sighed.

No matter how unscrupulous their choices in life, the famous enjoyed first-class treatment everywhere—even in the afterworld.

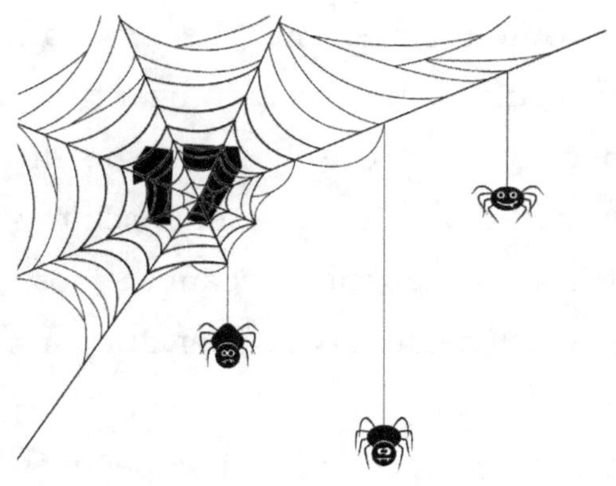

Admittedly, I entertained a status quo bias. I preferred that the conditions surrounding my workload stayed the same. My happiness and job satisfaction remained relatively protected when I worked with a manageable schedule, one I could keep up with effortlessly. No more souls needing spontaneous returns meant I enjoyed restful nights of uninterrupted sleep, the return of a hearty appetite, and, most of all, not feeling as drained as a phone bogged down with annoying apps.

The soul overload of the past several months had kept me on edge. I'd barely processed all the drama, leading me to a range of problems, from irritability to vision issues and mood swings.

But now, my chest cavity enjoyed a healthy fullness. I'd regained optimal health in a matter of days since the last soul return. My bones took on a luminous hue. I dared say

I glowed. Life had even complimented me: “Reaper, you look refreshed. Whatever you’re doing, keep doing it!”

How could I tell her it was precisely what she, in partnership with Death, had done that gave me back my mojo? No more bitter fights between them meant the boss didn’t rely on the bottle, which meant no more erratic soul returns.

Life and Death had developed new perspectives about each other’s roles in the game of existence. They understood what drove each other, and grew to support one another. Their interdependent relationship had blossomed to glorious new heights.

All these improvements allowed me to breathe easy again. At headquarters, I hummed and whistled and even swayed to the monotonous classical music playing through the speakers.

With a pep in my step, I pranced through the office like a new reaper.

My colleagues must’ve noticed, because they remarked on the depths of my empty eye sockets and the constant smile on my face bones. Someone even asked me if I’d gotten a new cloak, because it looked fantastic. I humbly replied, “This little thing? Nah, I just had time to sew on a few patches.”

With free time on my hand bones again, I decided to volunteer at the local spirit bank, where lost souls received encouragement and direction. I took every opportunity to nourish their souls with compliments, honest praise, and genuinely asked about their goals for the afterlife. Volunteering my time and energy was a meaningful way to give back to the afterworld community.

Existence was good. With my workload under control, I couldn't have asked for anything better.

One fine day, I rode an unremarkable soul to the other side. We gossiped about film stars and presidents. After the routine drop-off, I leisurely returned to the office. Another great, ordinary day.

As I basked in the delight of the status quo, my phone chirped. I dug into my cloak, pulled it out.

It was a text from Moe. I flinched a little.

It was unlike any other text I'd ever received from him or anyone else, leaving me slightly confused. The spirit guide's text was populated with several red SOS emojis, a bright yellow warning triangle emoji with an exclamation point inside, and more thick red exclamation points than I could count at a glance.

My initial confusion turned to outright disorientation. What in the afterworld was all this about?

Whenever Moe had texted me in recent times, it had been about souls who'd needed return passage. The spirit guide had no other reason to message me. But to my knowledge, I'd completed the last of the soul returns, leaving me free to do my job without burden.

I scanned the text, which indicated that one last soul had to be urgently returned. Moe had ended with, "Hurry!" and a frowning face emoji.

I clutched my phone firmly against my rib cage and leaned on the cubicle wall. My brow bones narrowed as I tried to make sense of the situation.

Moe had never expressed such heightened emotions. He was more like a laid-back spirit guide who couldn't care less about the fate of souls, which explained why he shrugged half-heartedly after pushing nearly every return client into the water while aiming for my boat. In fact, the only time he'd shown sincere respect was when the beautiful Leona Anci had arrived on the banks of eternity.

Something or someone had struck Moe enough to bring him to send a text of extreme urgency. My breath hitched.

Dreadfully curious, I grabbed my scythe and prepared to make my way across the river. It was a deathly silent ride, with no souls onboard to chitchat with or listen to complaints about trivial matters. The only sounds were the thoughts of intrigue running like mad through my skull.

Upon reaching the river's midpoint, I began to hear splashing and muffled yells coming from the banks of eternity. One of the voices sounded like the anguished cries of a cat. Instinctively, I rowed faster. My chest cavity heaved up and down. Sweat trickled down my face bones.

Visually, I couldn't make out anything from this distance, but I planted my feet bones and kept rowing, intending to respond to Moe's desperate call as quickly as I could.

The shouting match grew louder. As my boat glided closer to the banks, I noticed what looked like a dark blob jumping up and down. Moe stood beside it with his hands in front of his face, as if to shield himself.

I took a step back on the boat. It was a bizarre sight. The mighty Moe struggling with a dark, much shorter blob of circular proportions.

I continued to row, albeit slower and with deliberate caution.

The face on the dark blob appeared clearer. Its lips were colored black as night. Its eyes were lined with charcoal. Its black hair whiplashed across Moe's face, causing him to fall back.

My nasal cavities picked up an overpowering, cheap perfume, like a mix of bad chemicals. I pressed my hand bones over my face bones to avoid inhaling the offensive scent.

Moe scrambled to his knees, shouting, "No, no!"

Then he saw my boat approach. The spirit guide released a blood-curling scream, "Hurry, Reaper!"

But I paused.

The sight in front of me looked unnervingly familiar.

It took a minute, but it hit me like a cast-iron pan. My breath grew shaky. I shook my skull in denial. But no matter how I much I refused to believe what I saw, I couldn't avoid the fact. The soul that needed to be returned to the land of the living was none other than—Elvira!

She turned her head in my direction and waved. "Yoo-hoo, Reaper! I knew you'd come back to me, *amore mio*. We shall spend oodles of time in each other's embrace, you and I!"

I dropped my oar, covered my face bones, and fell to my knee bones.

My woeful cries bounced off the river's surface, as she lapped up my echoes of torment.

It couldn't be. Not Elvira, not again!

Thank you for reading

Crossing Over and Back: A Grim Reaper Comedy Adventure.

If you found this story spine-tinglingly delightful,

please consider leaving a review!

Other books in this series

A Morbid Obsession: A Grim Reaper Comedy Adventure

A Holly Jolly Reaper: A Grim Reaper Holiday Adventure

www.ingramcontent.com/pod-product-compliance
Lightning Source LLC
Chambersburg PA
CBHW071945190726
48293CB00004B/1362

* 9 7 8 1 9 5 6 4 9 6 5 2 9 *